Blues for
CHARLIE DARWIN

Books by **NAT HENTOFF**

Blues for CHARLIE DARWIN

Nat Hentoff

William Morrow and Company, Inc.
New York   1982

Grateful acknowledgment is made for permission to reprint the following:

On page 27, lines from the song "Steel A-Goin' Down" by Buell Kazee; permission for use granted by June Appal Recordings.

On page 58, lines from the poem "Ask Your Mama" from *Ask Your Mama: Twelve Moods for Jazz* by Langston Hughes, copyright © 1959, 1961 by Langston Hughes. Reprinted by permission of Alfred A. Knopf, Inc.

On page 185, lines from the song "Will the Circle be Unbroken" by A. P. Carter:

Copyright 1935 by Peer International Corporation
Copyright Renewed
Used by permission
All Rights Reserved

Library of Congress Cataloging in Publication Data

Hentoff, Nat.
    Blues for Charlie Darwin.

    I. Title.
PS3558.E575B5   813'.54   82–3484
ISBN 0–688–01260–4   AACR2

Printed in the United States of America

First Edition

1 2 3 4 5 6 7 8 9 10

BOOK DESIGN BY ELLEN LOGUIDICE

If a murder, anybody might have done it.
Burglary or pocket-picking wanted 'prenticeship.
Not so murder. We were all of us up to that.

Mr. Inspector, *Our Mutual Friend*

Wah Lee
Williams
2/87

San Francisco

1 In the dark of Indian summer, Shannon Leahy, going down into the subway, was talking to her editor and was getting nowhere, as if he were really there.

That's not a story, damn it. Some joint all of a sudden decides to have jazz dancing. Who the hell cares?

In her head, the editor's smooth, closed, black face said, *"Why, if you're not up to it, Miss Thing, I'll assign it elsewhere."*

Shannon was about to tell him—as she had not told him a half hour before—"Stick it!" when, like the Cheshire cat, her editor vanished and she became aware that, on the stairs, much too close to her, was this basketball player or descendant of a Watusi chief.

A sharp pain—as the thin gold chain dug into her neck by way of leave-taking. And it was gone! As was he, sprinting down to the bottom of the stairs, where he stopped for a moment, turned and smiled up at her. And was gone again.

Rubbing her neck, she opened her mouth to yell, and closed it. *Can you imagine? I'm too embarrassed to scream. "Gee, lady, you shouldn't be wearing no gold, even a little-bitty thing like that, outside, you know." I know. I know. I asked for it. It's my fault, right? No wonder the bastard was smiling. Jesus, what a place to live.*

She felt for the chain, to make sure it was really gone. And she saw the loping thief's black head, chopped from his body, on the subway platform, where she could kick it on to the tracks and then pick up her chain. But first, she had to buy a token to get in.

"You from the precinct?" asked the pockmarked ticket-taker at the Baked Alaska, a ground-floor club in Soho whose windows were painted black, except for a small, yellow neon sign in the shape of that sweet dessert.

"What the hell makes you think I'm a cop?" said Noah Green, a tall, bulky man of about fifty, with short brown hair and the face of an underexercised Saint Bernard. Detective Green thought of himself as moving about the city like The Shadow.

"You know what it is?" The Puerto Rican had just figured it out and was delighted that a cop would be the first to share in his discovery. "You know what it is? A man who can kill legal, he walks different. That's how I made you."

"Terrific." Green shoved the ticket at him. "Only you're wrong. I'm a wise guy. In from Cleveland on a job. Maybe I'll do two, smart-ass."

The Puerto Rican giggled. "Whatever you say, Captain. Only, you could have saved yourself the money."

Inside, the walls were mirrors; the white-leather bar revolved slowly, as did, even more slowly, a huge chandelier bathing the dancers in ever-changing, sickly hues. Green felt like throwing up.

He took a sketch out of his pocket—the thin, Oriental-looking face of a black man in his early thirties. He stared at it, looked at the faces in the wall mirror opposite the bar and, with the music getting too far into his head, tried to shake it out.

Goddamn composites. Must be two million people in this town who look like this cockroach. He was running out of the grocery store, right? So one citizen sees him from her twelfth-floor window across the street, and somebody else sees him zooming around the corner. What do they see? What can they see? And if I bring in the wrong guy from this cockamamie sketch, I'm the schmuck of the month. For Chrissake, Green, how could you miss? You had the goddamn composite!

He stuffed the paper in his pocket. Moving along the edges of the dance floor, looking for the composite murderer, Green shook his head. The ridiculously young black trumpet player was getting to him.

Son of a bitch can wail. Green stopped and lit a cigar, watching the spindly kid, eyes closed, face blank, leaping into "Tin Tin Deo," building climax after crackling climax with a huge, clear sound and a beat like a tidal wave.

Cupping his ear to get it all, Green suddenly turned as the dancers, rushing into each other, cleared a space where two men, each in his late twenties, each with a knife, watched the other with deadly expectation. And the music went on. The trumpet player, still expressionless, now had his eyes open, fixed on the knives, as he soared higher.

Hurling his bulk through the crowd, Green saw, just inside the frozen space, a tall, slender woman with long red hair. She was staring at the knives while writing, as if automatically, in a notebook.

"Back! Get the hell back!" Green roared, pushing her aside as he pulled his gun. Both men, a Puerto Rican and a black, dropped their knives with the Puerto Rican, wheedling, saying, "Hey, man, it's just a show, you know. Just tricks."

"We're going to give you a private rehearsal room," said the detective, motioning them hard toward the door.

"Hey, friend," a female voice snapped behind him. "Next time, watch your hands. You could have broken something with that shove. I heard you. I didn't have to get the message hand delivered."

The woman with the notebook was smiling. *Late twenties*, Green thought, *maybe a little more. Nice open Irish face, kind you can't trust.* She held up a press pass. "You got a job to do; I got a job to do."

"That thing doesn't entitle you to get killed, or to obstruct an officer."

"Which has the worse penalty?" she asked.

Green, embarrassed by the dead cigar in his mouth, moved past her, giving the black dueler a stiff poke toward the door.

"She turn you on, cop?" said the other prisoner.

Green threw his cigar on the floor. "Move," he growled. "Just move. Keep your mouth shut. Both of you."

"Nothing you can do to us," said the black prisoner. "All these people seen us as we go. Not a mark on us now. We be beat up once we go, you the one who did it."

"Everybody in this city is so fucking smart," Green said to the foul air, "so why do they keep getting their heads up their ass? And you," he said softly to the black man, "how many counts do you want to plead down from?"

The black man grimaced and did not say another word.

Having delivered the two dead-silent combatants to the uniformed force on the first floor of the precinct, Noah Green walked past a sign—*Corruption Can Be Reported to First Deputy Commissioner. Phone: 348–9200. Mail: Box 217, Brooklyn, N.Y. 11201*—and up a flight of stairs to a large, square room echoing with detectives talking to each other or on the telephone.

Sitting on the edge of a desk near the entrance was

Green's partner, a tall, bony, stiff-backed black detective in his late thirties, with a thick mustache.

"Didn't have time to make him, Sam." Green sat down heavily in a chair behind the desk. "If he was there. There was an unscheduled specialty act. Two assholes playing with knives."

"Got them downstairs?" Sam McKibbon asked.

"Yeah. Would it not be a grand thing to give them back their knives, lock them in a cell and, if God is good—"

McKibbon smiled. "I hear you. People who ain't even been born yet will have been spared who knows what from those mothers. Lovely idea. If I was running things, I'd give you a promotion for that one.

"Noah,"—McKibbon stood up—"I think we got the guy in the sketch we've been carrying around. I mean, he doesn't look anything like the sketch, so I figure we're on the right track."

"Wait a minute—" Green took out a cigar. "When did all this happen?"

"Your sweet man, Domingo, called around nine. First, he wasn't going to talk to me at all. Said he'd try to catch you later. That snitch really loves you, man. He only wants to make it with you. But I told him you and me were brothers and, besides, if he hung up on me, he'd be having breakfast on Rikers Island tomorrow and did he remember what that shit tastes like?"

McKibbon took out a pipe and slowly filled it with tobacco from a nearly exhausted blue package of Edgeworth. "Domingo," he continued, "had a name to go with the homicides in the *bodega,* and he had an address for the name. This is the guy, he tells me. *The* guy who got the old man in the head, and when mama screamed, shot her in the mouth and steps over her to clean out the register. Wham, bam, thank you, ma'am."

Green nodded. "Scumbag of the week."

"I dunno," said McKibbon. "We still got three days left. Anyway, Domingo says he don't know nothin about the other two who came into the *bodega* with this cockroach, but he's sure of this one. He's never seen the guy himself, but it's the real stuff."

"How can he be so sure?" Green looked at his partner.

"Privileged information. He won't say where he got it. Domingo says we could crush his balls all night long, but he won't say. He doesn't want to walk around without a tongue. That'd be very hard for a Puerto Rican, he says."

Green rubbed his nose. "All we got to go with is what a snitch says on the phone." He smiled. "Seems to me I've heard that tune before. Must have been Bird or somebody like that."

"Ah," McKibbon watched a perfect smoke ring leave his pipe, "but this is the most truthful, loyal, industrious, if not courageous, snitch in the West. If I've heard you say that once, I've heard you say it twice."

"Yeah,"—Green knocked lightly on the desk— "Domingo is something else. But listen, you say the guy Domingo gave you is *here?*"

"Right. Stubblefield's the name. Preceded by Frank."

"Where is he?"

"In the lieutenant's office," McKibbon said, "reading the commander's wall of commendations. The Randazzo Files, starring Fortunato Randazzo as himself."

"What the hell'd you bring Stubblefield in on, crossing the street against a red light?"

"Why, Noah," McKibbon knocked the ashes out of his pipe. "Mr. Stubblefield is not in custody for anything. He came here, as a good citizen, on my invitation, to volunteer whatever he may know concerning the unfortunate turn of events last night in that grocery store. Since all *I* have at the moment is what your Domingo said on the phone, I can't do any more than appeal to Mr. Stubblefield's civic responsibility. He is not a suspect."

Green grunted. "Stubblefield has been told he's not a suspect?"

"He asked," McKibbon answered. "What could I tell him? The truth. Sort of. There's nothing we could go to a judge with that he'd listen to, right? So I told Stubblefield he's not a suspect. So, since he's not even a suspect, and certainly not in custody, he doesn't need a lawyer, and we don't have to warn him about shit."

"Jesus," Green said, "it's a damn good thing the Supreme Court doesn't do any fieldwork. Why did this Stubblefield *volunteer* to come in?"

"He's on parole," McKibbon said. "Nothing in this world he'd rather do than cooperate with us. Except he doesn't know a thing. Not one fucking thing. That's what he tells me. So it's up to our master interrogator. If you can't get anything out of him, we're going to have to send him home. But, if you're really cooking tonight, there's nothing a lawyer can do later if this agonized soul—who could have walked out of here any time he wanted to—had to get a terrible burden off his mind. Mama lying there with her nose shot off, and half of papa's head oozing onto the bananas. I haven't read the *Law Journal* yet today, but I think a confession still holds up if it's truly, truly voluntary. And that's your specialty, Noah."

Green took out his cigar. "Who knows about Domingo's call?"

"Just you and me and Domingo," his partner said.

"Is the room set up?"

"Yes, sir," McKibbon said. "Just two chairs. Nothing between you and him. As if you were lovers."

"Same principle." Green lit his cigar. "That's why they call it screwing."

It was a small room, next to Lieutenant Randazzo's much more ample quarters. The walls, like those of the squad room outside, were pale green, and there were no windows.

Stubblefield, who looked to be in his mid-forties, was short, stocky, coffee-colored, with a moon face and sparse straight hair. He wore a dark brown suit, yellow shirt and dark green tie. He tried to lean back in the steel chair, played with a button on his jacket and then, taking a deep breath, Stubblefield straightened up and looked straight at Green.

He knew nothing about the murders, except, from the *New York Post,* that they had taken place. He had never been inside the *bodega.* He lived ten blocks away. And he had no idea why the police thought he had any information.

"What do you do for a living?" Green asked amiably.

"I work in a record store. Jazz Gallery."

"Yeah, I know the place. You hear the new Sonny Rollins?"

Stubblefield nodded. "Cat's always taking chances. I admire that. In his line of work, I mean."

"Like Miles used to be." They discussed the sputtering career of Miles Davis, went on to Clifford Brown and had begun a comparison of Betty Carter and Sarah Vaughan when Stubblefield said, "You know, this isn't going anywhere. I can hear your wheels moving. You guys make a study of perpetrators, but you never figure that some perpetrators are studying you. Ex-perpetrator, in my case."

Green offered Stubblefield a cigar, which was declined. "That's a long, busy sheet you got."

"No violence on it, right? But like I was saying, *Criminal Interrogation and Confessions,* Inbau and Reid—

'Ask the subject innocuous questions that have no bearing whatever on the matter under investigation. As a rule the subject will answer such questions, and then gradually the examiner may start in with questions pertaining to the offense.' "

"No shit," Green said. "Before you go, I'd like to write down the name of that book."

"Look," Stubblefield said, "it is very much against my best interest to antagonize you, okay? But I wanted to save us both a lot of time. I do not know anything about those killings. I don't know who told you I did, and why he told you. Maybe it's an old friend from the inside who thinks he owes me something. But you're not going to tell me who it was. You don't have anything to hold me on, or you would have. So what can I say to you? If I hear anything, I'll let you know. You don't believe that, but now I got to try to find out what went down because somebody's trying to hang it on me. So, can I go home or do I call a lawyer?"

Green stood up. "I believe you," he said. "Your wheels go so fast that you figure I'm just conning you another way. But, as we get to know each other, Frank, we'll establish some trust. Or at least some respect. Here's my card, when you want to call."

The ex-perpetrator took out a black pinseal wallet and put in the card. Looking up, he said to Green, "It's *mine*. Paid for."

Green walked him to the stairs as Sam McKibbon, expressionless, looked on. Back in the squad room, Green said to his partner, "I fucked up. I don't think he did it anyway, but I never got into any kind of groove. Maybe I've been working too hard."

"Couldn't reach him, huh?"

"Sam, the little creep started analyzing my technique. He told me what I was doing, and the fucker was right."

McKibbon tried not to laugh. "If I promise not to tell the lieutenant about this, will you promise not to smoke those damn stogies in the car? Head's supposed to be clear when you get to the crime scene."

"That's the problem," Green slumped into a chair. "My head's not working the way it used to. Can't sustain the focus. Or something."

"If you will excuse my being vulgar,"—McKibbon put his feet up on the desk—"no man can be without a piece of ass as long as you have been without a piece of ass and not have a fucked-up head."

Green bit at his cigar. "It was a lot worse when I was married."

Outside, in the cold December night, Stubblefield looked up and down the street. It was empty. He went over to a parked police car and spat on the windshield.

2 A little before midnight, on Waverly Place in Greenwich Village, the detective, looking in the window of the long, narrow Ferdinand Morton Memorial Bookstore, saw that the proprietor was alone. Black, wiry, her eyes large and deep, she waved at him.

Green opened the door, came up to the counter, and she kissed him lightly on the cheek. "It's late, Emma," he said. "You're asking for it."

"Nobody knocks off a bookstore, Noah," she smiled. "We have a reasonably bright criminal class. They're not going to waste their time here, especially with the liquor store two doors away."

Green sighed. "They might want *you*. Some of them have eyes for more than bread. Listen, I'm not going to argue with you. Only people I know more stubborn than you are the lieutenant and that hillbilly you put up with."

"It's when Bama has a gig that I stay this late," she said. "Awful lonely at home with just that mean dog for company. I really hate that Merle Haggard."

Green laughed. "Why don't you get a black dog to keep him in his place? Call him Coleman Hawkins. Where's the hillbilly fiddling tonight?"

"College in Jersey."

"A lot of those young women going to be looking hard at that long man."

Emma stretched. The suppleness of the strong, slender body made Green look away. "That's the one thing in this whole world, Noah, that I don't have to worry about."

"You're wrong about being safe here alone at night. Or anytime." He was looking through a tableful of remainders. "But you're right about that. Never saw two people who fit together like you and Bama. Anyway, do me a mitzvah. Lock up."

"Half an hour," she said. "Got to finish making out the list for the next mailing. There's a Chester Himes I don't think you have."

"Put it aside for me."

"Don't you want to know the title?"

"If I have it, I'll give it to Sam for Christmas. He's never read any Himes, can you imagine that? Listen, from now on, at least bring that Merle Haggard with you."

Emma laughed. *"Nobody* would come in with that monster here. Hey, Noah, why don't *you* lock up and go home?"

"Restless. It's like that some nights. If I went home, I'd go right out again."

"Uh-huh," said the bookstore owner as she watched him leave, pause outside to peer at a new book on John Coltrane in the window, wave at her and walk down the street.

Emma shook her head. *Big, hard Noah. Until you look into those eyes. Saddest eyes I ever saw. Not only sad. Hungry. Wanting some kind of woman who never was, never will be. Like my daddy. He was always wanting too. Never found out what. Sure wasn't mama.*

Emma stuck her tongue out at the list of books for the mailing. *Hold on.* She looked into the night. *If something happened to Bama, that man might come on. It'd take*

Noah a long time, but he could make a move. What would I do then? Leave him wanting, I guess. Maybe not.

She waved the speculation away. *Nothing's going to happen to Bama. I'm going to live to be ninety-four, and he's going to live to be ninety-five. And then we'll do it again. Without that Merle Haggard.*

It was the next Monday. The call came in at three in the morning. From the husband. He had gone to bed early; nothing had disturbed him until he got up to go to the bathroom, saw the light still on in the kitchen, and there on the floor was—

"Our newest client." McKibbon looked out the car window. "One advantage we got is we never have to solicit new business."

Green grunted as they turned into a small, narrow street in the West Village. A uniformed cop and half a dozen civilians stood in front of a brownstone.

"Shit," Green said. "Reporters."

"Corpse must be white," his partner said.

Frowning, Green got out of the car. McKibbon went over to the cop.

"Detective Green," the tall redheaded reporter stepped in front of him.

He gave no indication he recognized the sunny mick face, let alone the figure. "How do you know it's Detective Green?"

"It's not?" She was amused. "I have it from usually reliable sources."

He glanced at the cop talking to McKibbon. "Watch out for sources who carry guns. How'd you find out about this?"

Shannon Leahy grinned. "Guglielmo."

"What? Who?"

"Guglielmo Marconi."

"Yeah, but where would radio have been without David Sarnoff?"

Green turned away, following McKibbon up the steps.

"We'll be waiting for you, Detective Green," she said cheerily.

He turned back. "Don't waste your time. I never speak to the press about a case until and if the perpetrator has been sentenced. You got that, lady?"

"Hey, Noah,"—she waited until he was on the top step—"the name is not lady. The name is Leahy. Shannon Leahy. *Journal.* Keep it in mind."

As they maneuvered through the partly open door, McKibbon said, "Next to judges, reporters are the worst assholes there are. At least judges stay put."

"I'll wear her down," Green smiled.

"How do you mean that?"

Only the corpse was in the large, spotless, brightly lit kitchen. And a uniformed cop with his hands in his pockets.

McKibbon nodded approvingly. "Where'd you learn that?" he said to the cop, a thickset, black-haired man with a graying mustache.

"Lieutenant Riordan, when he was in the precinct. 'If you keep your hands in your pockets until the investigator comes,' he'd say, 'you'll not be touching anything.' "

"How'd you get in?" Green asked sharply.

"The husband. I knocked, up high on the door. He let me in. But he says it wasn't locked, although he says he locked it himself before he went to bed. I left it ajar so you wouldn't have to use the knob."

"And the sainted lieutenant would say to *us,*" McKibbon chanted softly, looking sideways at Green, " 'Take note not only of what you see, but also of what you don't see that normally should be there.' Like—"

"Can we knock off the catechism?" Green said sourly, looking at the body from the doorway. Lying on her right side was a trim, athletic-looking woman in her early forties, about five feet, four inches with Indian-black hair. In her back was a bone-handled knife plunged almost to the hilt. There were many other incisions—on the face, neck, chest, thighs and buttocks.

Stepping carefully over the blood, McKibbon knelt down and looked at the passionate handiwork. "Whoever did that didn't want to ever stop." He bent closer, focusing on her forearms, palms and fingers. There were no cuts in any of those places.

"No defense wounds." McKibbon stood up.

"Where the hell are the crime-scene guys?" Green asked the uniformed cop.

"Soon. They had another call to make. You know how stretched out those guys are. The husband wants to talk to you."

"He in shape to talk?" Green asked.

"He doesn't do nothing but," said the cop. "He's not exactly grief-stricken, but, then, Lieutenant Riordan used to say you really can't tell much by how the near and dear behave right after the unfortunate incident. It isn't real to them yet, you know."

Green glared at him. "Why don't you take your hands out of your pockets and put them in your mouth? Both hands!"

"Burton Ginsburg is the name." The tall, spare, sandy-haired widower held his hand out to McKibbon, then to Green, and suddenly stopped, staring at the corpse. He moved a hand toward her, drew it back and vomited on the floor.

"My apologies," Ginsburg said. "I'll get some paper towels."

"No," Green shook his head, turning away. "You don't know what else you might be picking up. Another room we can go to?"

Ginsburg led the way to a small study. On all four walls bookshelves reached to the ceiling. Each row, Green noted, was so orderly as to be quite depressing. Green glanced out the window and saw what might have been a friendly or a mocking wave from Shannon Leahy. He did not respond.

"We're sorry to intrude," Green began.

"No problem," the widower said. "What just happened in there—well, I guess it wasn't real to me until just then."

There was a sound from McKibbon, which he hoped resembled a cough. As Green started the questioning, his partner, hearing voices at the front door, rose.

"I want pictures of everything," Green said. "The ceiling. Everything. *Clear* pictures."

"Jees," said McKibbon as he was leaving, "and I thought you were all for affirmative action."

The Ginsburgs had been married nearly six years. The survivor was an associate professor of English at New York University. Kathleen Ryan Ginsburg had been a free-lance editor, part-time copy editor and sometime typist.

"She had a manuscript due in the morning," the professor said. "A novel. A long one. When I went to bed about twelve, she had a fair amount of typing left to do."

"Did she often work late?" Green asked.

"She was a night person. Usually an all-night person. I am not. And besides, she often had rush jobs."

"Where did she work?"

"In the kitchen. The best light in the house, she said."

"She drink?"

"Coffee. Incessantly."

"Any idea who might have killed her?"

The professor looked startled. "I hadn't even begun to think of that. A burglar, I suppose. Who else? Certainly no one we knew."

Green took out a cigar and lit it. "I hope you don't mind my asking, but did the two of you get on okay?"

Ginsburg stared at the cigar.

"Oh," said the detective. "That bother you?"

"I'm afraid it does. We never allowed smoking in this house. It made us ill. About the only thing we ever agreed on."

Green squashed out the cigar.

"You'll find out," the professor said, "so I'll tell you now. She despised me. She said I was weak because I am nonviolent. Indeed I am. All the way, I served three years as nonreligious conscientious objector in the Second World War. She said nonviolence was a lace curtain way of hiding cowardice. Or, as she put it, no balls. Sometimes she would hit me in the stomach full force."

"You never broke?"

"Never. My whole life would be a lie if I were to put a hand to anyone. We were at odds on other things too. I am a vegetarian, she is not. She thought psychoanalysis utterly stupid, and I have been in therapy. She loved country music, and I cannot abide all that sodden whining."

"And in bed?" Green asked softly.

"I don't think I have to answer that."

"Okay."

"There had been none of that for four years or so."

"Why did you stay together?"

"I doubt if you'll understand this, but we also loved each other."

"It's not the first marriage of that kind I ever heard of. In and out of literature."

McKibbon was back. "It's a good crew. I laid it out for them. Meanwhile, I looked around a little. Back door locked. All windows locked. No attempts at forced entry anywhere, including the front door."

"I guess you'll be giving me my rights at this point?" Ginsburg looked at Green.

"No, sir. Except for the cliché that everybody is a suspect, we do not, in those terms, have a suspect as yet."

"In that case," Ginsburg rose, speaking just as calmly as before, "although I thought I was up to this, I would rather answer the rest of your questions tomorrow. I think I will be able to focus better then." He gave Green his phone number at the university.

"You're going to class tomorrow?" Green asked.

"I have my obligations."

Green also stood up. "Thank you, professor. Oh, by tomorrow, would you make a list—an annotated list—of all the friends and acquaintances of your wife, including those you held in common? The nature of the relationships, and information about everyone on the list, including addresses and phone numbers."

"It won't be long," Ginsburg said. "We did not socialize much."

"That's all right. We're only looking for one person."

In the car, McKibbon coughed warningly as Green started to light a cigar.

"Shit," his partner said, "you're really holding me to that promise?"

"Hell, everybody in the department knows that Noah Green never breaks his word. And all the snitches in all the boroughs know that too."

"What do you think?" Green shoved the matches back in his pocket.

"Too fucking easy," McKibbon said. "No break-in. He tells you what a foul marriage it was. The only thing missing is his confession. I don't like it."

"On the other hand, it sure could be him."

"Not in your gut you don't think that."

"No." Green felt very tired. "But I learned a long time ago to be very wary of my instincts. They can be working for the other side."

"Hey, what are we going to tell the lieutenant?" McKibbon was smoothing his mustache.

"Until we canvass, we tell him the professor is *numero uno* but we don't have enough yet to take him in, and besides, he's the kind of guy who'll break only if you let him think he's off the hook. And that's the truth."

"You tell him that, Noah. When I'm not there." McKibbon stopped for a red light. "Hey, she also got whanged on the back of the head. They don't know yet by what. But that's not what did her in."

"I know,"—Green chewed on his unlit cigar—"I saw. You ever see a burglar cut anybody up like that?"

"Yeah. A nut. You think all burglars got all their marbles, just because they're not robbers?"

3 The dog, which some timorous citizens might have taken for a wolf, was cream in color, baleful of eye and had devil's ears. He growled noncommittally as the fiddle player opened the door as softly as he could.

"Good night, Merle Haggard," Alabama Dixon whispered with as much authority as a whisper can hold. The dog turned around, went into the kitchen and lay down in his corner near the stove.

"It's good morning, Bama," a voice came from the living room. "Midnight's been here and gone."

The tall, lean musician with soft, light brown hair, light blue eyes and a face that looked as if it had been carved out of hardwood, went into the room. He put the fiddle case on the window seat, moved to the rocking chair next to the bay window where Emma was sitting and kissed her on top of the head.

"Little old Jew banjo player—"

"Jewish," she said.

"Still don't know what the difference is. Anyway, he couldn't be no more than sixteen goddamn years old. He sat in. Never been south of Atlantic City, but Jesus, can he pick! Might even scare Earl Scruggs some. So after the gig, we went to the dorms and just kept on going. Little bugger knows everything ever been put on a record. He knows more Buell Kazee than I do. Remember 'Steel A-Goin' Down?' "

Bama stood in front of her, and in a high, lonesome voice sang:

In the evening burns a light soft and low
In that little shanty where I long to go.
Steel a-goin' down, and my hammer's gettin' heavy.
I'm a gettin' weary. I'm a goin' home.

Emma smiled and nodded. "Can he *sound* like that?"

"No, thank God," Bama said. "Jew boy got a voice like he was being chased by a pack of hounds. But damn it, Emma, how do you figure he picks that banjo so *southern?*"

"Can't keep nothing to yourself anymore. We're all one big lousy family. Want a drink, Bama?"

"Sure. A big one. And that ain't all I want."

"I know, but I see you drifting. You don't want to fall asleep right in the middle. I'll be here when you get up. Store can wait."

Bama sprawled on the bold Navajo blanket covering the couch. "Anything new?" he yawned.

"No. Noah came by tonight. There's a hole in that man, Bama."

"Yeah. Getting bigger. But he'll keep patching himself up. Noah's a proud man before he's anything else. Why, he's tougher than my daddy."

"Your daddy," Emma said, "drank himself to death."

"Never complained though. So many things eating him all the way through, but he never complained to no one. That's what counts."

"Where does it count, Bama?"

But he was asleep.

His big thumb squashing the alarm button, Green eased his leaden body out of the bed, brushing the *Daily News,* open to a page of comics, onto the floor, where it joined his pants and shoes. In yesterday's shorts, he moved into the bathroom, closed the door, looked in the mirror at the used face, the deep crosshatched bags under the eyes, the ridiculously small chin, and said to his derisive familiar, "She's probably married. Sure, she's married. A body like that, a smile like that, a voice like Margaret Sullavan's. Why shouldn't she be married? Or she's divorced, being banged by half the reporters in town. Just like a *shikseh*. You'd get a disease from her. Anyway, I bet she's an anti-Semit. Leahy? *Vo den?*"

Fifteen minutes later, coming out of the apartment building on the upper West Side, Green saw the wheelchairs and checked his watch. 8:40. Right on the dime. A slight young man, maybe twenty, moving himself forward by turning the back wheels; next to him a chubby young woman, maybe a year younger, doing the same. Chatting, smiling, strapped textbooks on their laps, they had six blocks to go before Columbia. When his week turned around and he slept mornings, Green regretted not seeing them.

Walking toward the garage, he saw, against the window of a stationery store, a wraith of a man, hunched over, walking as if he were listening to an utterly fascinating conversation. Somewhere past forty, though how far past it was hard to say, he wore a light brown corduroy jacket, a green corduroy cap, a pink, buttoned-down Brooks Brothers shirt, chino pants from the same source, and carried a much weathered green book bag over his shoulder. His features were those of an attractive but dead baby.

They did not acknowledge each other. But instead of continuing toward the garage, Green followed the little man until he went into a coffee shop near the university. Green also entered, found a booth in the back, and the wraith soon materialized opposite him. Neither spoke until the waitress took their orders and left.

The wraith smiled, showing perfect pale purple teeth. "You're the first to see this shade," he said. "That makes seven now. Once I get it on the market, the whole damn country will be smiling."

"What about your schlong? Does it match?"

Crocker Whipple laughed delicately. "You are really so stuck on the flypaper, Noah. My set's been doing that for years. Wanna see?"

"No, I'm on a diet. Do you know anything?"

"Not yet. But I rather thought you'd ask me to look deep into the living memory of Kathleen Ryan Ginsburg, so I have begun my historical research."

The waitress brought two orders of bacon and eggs, coffee for Green and tea for Whipple. When Whipple smiled broadly in gratitude, her hand went to her throat in dismayed surprise. "Next time I'm in, dear," he said through a grin, "I'll show you the jade. It's quietly stunning."

"You summoned me,"—Whipple speared a slice of bacon as the waitress hurried away—"because you want to find out if she was AC/DC. Why did that prurient thought dance into your head?"

"No special reason. Isn't nearly everybody AC/DC by now?"

"You are so witty. You really are. I wager most people don't know that about you. All they see is that dour exterior. Ah, Noah, some day there will be no more of these back-street encounters. Some day, we shall go arm in arm down Fifth Avenue together."

"Better yet," said Green, rising, "I'll take you to *shul* with me next Yom Kippur."

Even when seated, Lieutenant Fortunato Randazzo

looked like a tackle barely waiting for the snap. A large, solid man in his late forties, with thick, black, curly hair, quick gray eyes and restless hands, he was leafing through a file of the unredeemed dead, stopping on occasion to take some sour balls from a large apothecary jar on his desk.

"A hunk of meat." Randazzo pushed a photograph toward Green and McKibbon. "No head, no arms, no legs. The Hudson can't wash it up at Midtown North. Oh no, it has to land here and screw up my clearance rate. It makes you appreciate a mob hit. At least there's a *face* I can look at."

"We've got better odds with the hunk of meat," McKibbon said.

"That's because,"—Randazzo leaned over the desk and dug his forefinger into McKibbon's shoulder—"you guys got it in your mind that those particular kind of dagos got magic powers when it comes to killing. Shit, those out-of-town beauties, they don't vanish off the face of the fuckin' earth once they do the thing. We give up too easy. I'm gonna show you yo-yos. Next wise guy that gets it, *I'm* gonna handle the case. I know how they think; I grew up with greaseballs like that. Just like you," —he looked at McKibbon—"you know how the bad *shvartzehs* think better than we do."

"Yassuh." McKibbon pressed on the bowl of his pipe. "All I got to do, whenever I'm stuck, is dip into the collective racial unconscious."

"Damn it!" Randazzo banged his hand on the desk. "I dream of that hunk of meat. The fuckhead that threw that in my lap, he's laughing at me—he goes to bed laughing at me. Gentlemen, do you know the last thing that's going to go through my mind when I finally come to the end of me?"

"That hunk of meat," McKibbon said brightly.

"No!" Randazzo bellowed. "No! What will be poisoning my last breath of life are other failures, worse failures. The failure to lead and inspire my men. Like on the afternoon of the very next day after a brutal murder of a married woman in her own home, two of my men are sitting in my office and they let me go on and on about anything but what *they* should be telling me. You haven't got a damn thing, right?"

"Not for an arrest, no," Green said. "But—"

"No prints on the knife." Randazzo tapped his fingers on the desk. "No prints anywhere in the house, except Kathleen's and the professor's, right? Right. No marks on the windows, which were locked. Back door locked. Front door not locked. The professor says he locked it. He could also have unlocked it. Why am I doing all the talking?"

"You think I should have brought him in?" Green asked.

"You caught the case," Randazzo said. "I didn't."

"That one would have called a lawyer,"—Green eyed the sour balls—"and that would have been the end of any questioning. That's a bird we have to work on slow."

Randazzo took a sour ball out of the jar and threw it, hard, at Green, whose hand closed over it. "Well, we'll never know whether you could have cracked him right away." The lieutenant shook his fist at the picture of the torso. "But you may be right. You better be right." He looked at McKibbon. "What about the canvassing?"

"Vinnie started about eight this morning," McKibbon said. "Nothing yet. Some of the folks on that street, either they go to work awful early or they come home awful late. The others, nothing disturbed their sleep. And they know nothing about the Ginsburgs. Very unsociable couple. So unsociable the folks on the street almost never saw them together. Noah and I are going back tonight."

Randazzo handed the apothecary jar to McKibbon, who shook his head.

"And I checked out the widower." McKibbon took out his pipe. "Ginsburg did time all right, but only what he said he did. Two years, eleven months. Refused induction. Refused alternative service, refused food for a while. But then Mr. Ginsburg decided he had no right to die while the world was at war and in need of peacemakers. This decision was not put to a vote among his buddies in the jug. If it had been, it is likely that Mr. Ginsburg would not be in our thoughts this morning."

"Not popular with the other yellow-bellies?" Randazzo asked.

"His fellow pacifists wanted to strangle him. The three I reached couldn't really explain why. They just *wanted* to. Makes sense to me. That is one clammy cat."

"And you?" Randazzo turned to Green.

"I heard the professor's lecture this morning. No way of telling there'd been a death in the family. And he gave me that list of her friends and acquaintances. A big seven. She hadn't seen any of them for a couple of months, he says. She worked all the time, or read, or went to the main library or snapped at him. Then he had another class, but Mr. Ginsburg and I are going to be seeing a lot of each other."

"Maybe you should enroll," Randazzo said, "in case you need an advanced degree to go into another line of work."

Ignoring the advice, Green told the lieutenant of the assignment he had given Crocker Whipple. "He can find out things that nobody straight can."

Randazzo grunted. "Dirty stuff. I hate using fags; I hate giving them any kind of legitimacy."

"He's reliable," Green said. "He hasn't thrown us any curves."

"How can you say?" Randazzo rose to give fuller voice to his feelings. "How can you say that a guy who *shtups* another guy up the ass is reliable? One thing, Noah, any time you meet with that fag and then you're coming in here, wash your hands first, all right?"

Randazzo walked over to the window, turned around and said, "Gentlemen, under normal circumstances—a term that is a laugh and a half here—you are making the more or less correct initial moves, but I do not get the sense that you are breaking your balls on behalf of the deceased and on behalf of your beloved commander.

"Listen!" Randazzo had seated himself again and was leaning across the desk. "This is not a homicide on Avenue A. This is a lady chopped up in a neighborhood where you got at least a couple Criminal Court judges, a judge in the Appellate Division, a shitload of psychiatrists, writers, lawyers and what not. And it's where the Mayor still keeps an apartment.

"We can get another clearance rate of seventy-one percent this year, but if we do not clear *this* case, it won't matter. We will all look like shit, especially me, because the press and City Hall will be watching *this* case, and checking off their fucking calendars. *Fashtaist?*" The lieutenant looked at Green.

"I don't think like that," Green said, "and you know it."

"I don't give a fuck what you think," Randazzo said calmly. "No offense. You got egalitarian principles. All corpses should get equal treatment. In my position, I got the real world to deal with, and at times like this, the real world takes me up by the short hairs and reminds me where the priorities are."

Sam McKibbon knocked the ashes out of his pipe. "Those priorities never change color, do they?"

"Bull—shit!" Randazzo shouted. "If Kathleen Ryan Ginsburg had been a *shvartzeh* and had been killed in that house in that neighborhood, I would not be saying one fucking different thing. When are you going to learn it's all about class? Not color. You understand I used the term *shvartzeh* affectionately."

"God help me, Lieutenant," said McKibbon, "I really think you did. All right. I'm going to think of Kathleen as the right kind of *shvartzeh.*"

"And what's going to goose *you?*" Randazzo looked at Green.

"I told you, I don't play this game. I break my balls for all of them." And Green walked out of the office.

"What the hell's eating *him?*" Randazzo asked.

"What the hell do *shvartzehs* know about what bothers you people?" McKibbon said from the door.

4 Green, in the squad room, was looking out the window at all the good citizens hurrying home in the early winter darkness. He reminded himself he didn't envy them.

"I figure we start knocking around seven-thirty," Sam McKibbon said. "They've had dinner, they've had the news, and we'll be the movie."

His partner nodded. The phone rang. "Green here."

"Connie would like to buy you a drink," said the softly curving, vanilla voice of Crocker Whipple on the other end.

"That's it? That all you got?"

"Why, that invitation should tell you volumes," Whipple said. "Connie hasn't changed her policy, you know. Cocks get in only by special dispensation. Into the room, I mean."

"Okay. Find out anything about the survivor among *your* melancholy people?"

"Not a ripple yet, but I have only begun to sniff. I'll be in touch, dear."

Green reached for a cigar. "Don't let your public parts get stuck in the glory hole, Crocker," he chortled into the phone.

"That tickles you, doesn't it?" Whipple said. "Will you let me know it's you in the next stall?"

Smiling, Green hung up and turned to his partner. "I think we got a lead on Kathleen. Connie wants to see me."

McKibbon nodded. "Well, that figures. If Kathleen wasn't twisted before she married the professor, a year or so with him would have done it."

The phone rang. "Green here."

"Shannon Leahy from the *Journal*, remember?"

"What can I do for you?"

"It's the other way around. I may have something on the Ginsburg killing. It's not just background stuff, but it may be of use to you."

"I thought you people didn't want to be an arm of the police," Green couldn't resist saying.

"I had a cop in the family," she said. "But to hell with it."

"Hold on. I also thought reporters were quick with the repartee without taking it serious. I'm going out now, but could you meet me around eleven-thirty? Rafferty's. Seventh Avenue and Twenty-first Street. A crummy bar, jukebox and television all on at once."

"I'll be carrying an early edition of the paper."

"Oh, I'll know you. I never forget a dangerous face." Green hung up. "Or ass."

"Huh?" McKibbon looked at him.

"That reporter from the *Journal*—what's her name, Leahy?—says she may have something on Kathleen. God is being good to us tonight. Which means he'll really screw us tomorrow."

"But now you're going down to Connie's?" McKibbon asked.

"Yeah. Before she changes her mind. She's no great talker, you know. You can handle the canvassing?"

"Sure." McKibbon leaned back in his chair. "I'm beginning to feel a little bit sorry for that *pisher* professor. If that's the way it comes down with Kathleen, he's going to feel like some schmuck, so to speak. Can't you see the two of them on the front page of the *Post?* DIKE DICED. WAS MARRIED TO NYU PROFESSOR."

McKibbon allowed himself a quick smile. "So where we gonna connect?"

"Call me at Rafferty's," Green said. "Eleven-thirty or so."

A young undercover cop, looking quite convincingly like a bum, a bottle in a paper bag visible in a pocket of his thin, greasy coat, walked over to McKibbon's desk. "Hey," he said, pointing to Lieutenant Randazzo's empty office, "you guys seen the new one?"

Green and McKibbon went to the door, and on a far wall hung with pictures, plaques and adages, there was a small framed typescript:

IF GOD HAD WANTED PERMISSIVENESS,
HE WOULD HAVE GIVEN THE TEN SUGGESTIONS.

Green had expected the usual softly grooving piano and bass behind the usual rail-thin singer with blank eyes and a low, private voice that gave him a hard-on. Even though he knew what she was. All right, maybe especially because he knew what she was. This night, though, while he was still half a block away from Connie's, Green heard a hard, gritty, shouting tenor saxophone. It was moving in and out of the chords and, by the time he came to the door, the horn was stomping and smashing the chords so he wasn't sure anymore what the tune was. It was just sound. Ugly screeching sound coming from a saxophone looking bigger than the crisp, frizzy-haired girl behind it, her eyes shut, her thin body crouching, as if for some kind of kill.

Connie's was a small, square, softly lit room, its most distinctive fixture a burnished red-mahogany bar that matched the two women bartenders. At the end of the bar stood Connie, deep black, a little over six feet, her aquiline face looking like a figurehead on a pirate ship.

"I sure miss Ben Webster," Green shouted in her ear.

Connie laughed. "Don Byas too. Only Lockjaw's left with that *big*, round sound, and he's older than we are."

The set was over, and Green applauded enthusiastically for the respite.

"But you got to adjust if you want to make it in the night," Connie said. "Still Cutty Sark?" She looked toward the bartender.

"No, thanks. Club soda. I decided to be an example to the younger men on the force."

"Louts!" Connie spit out the word.

"Why do you say that?" Green was looking at the tight rear end of the ferocious tenor player. "A lot of them have more education than we did."

"They're ice cold, Noah. Your generation, at least there's something in your eyes. These scumbags, their eyes are empty. They're like from some other planet. The natives here aren't human to them."

Green laughed. "They're from the planet of Long Island."

"Fucking right," Connie said. "They live in those chickenshit towns, and they can't wait to get out of here to go back to Lilac Road where everybody looks like their own pasty selves. Jesus, how can you associate with such pods?"

Green sipped the club soda.

"Say something, damn it." Connie put a long finger on the detective's arm.

"Kathleen Ryan Ginsburg."

"I thought you'd never ask. Come on." She motioned Green to follow her into a small office behind the bar. There were two straight-backed chairs, a steel table on which a turntable, stereo receiver and tape deck sat and, in opposite corners, two ancient KLH speakers. On the floor were several large piles of LPs.

"I'm not especially demonstrative, Noah," Connie said as they sat down, "but I want you to know I very much appreciate what you did with the liquor authority. Christ, I had no idea the little motherfucker was fourteen. Can't tell anybody's age anymore. Not in this town. You see a baby in a carriage, and the cocksucker's dealing."

"Kathleen," Green said.

"She used to come by. Once a week or so. A hunter. Whoever she wanted, she wanted so bad, it was a drag. Almost pathetic. It got to where the regulars acted as if she wasn't there. And that made her spit. She had all the soul of that piece of poison playing tenor. You play what you are, and that sound is exactly what that bitch is. Comes from Texas. It's amazing Lyndon Johnson didn't blow us all up."

"Kathleen," Green said.

"I banned her," Connie said. "A month ago. I'd get a bad feeling in my gut as soon as she walked in. I don't have to be uncomfortable in my own place. What the hell's capitalism for?"

"How'd she react?"

"I never saw her again until she hit the papers. I didn't know her name until then."

"Hear anything about what she was doing outside, before and after the banning?"

Connie looked at him. "I don't owe you any information about what goes on outside my place."

"You didn't read the fine print." Green took out a cigar. "You mind?"

"I really don't know anything," Connie said coolly.

"Is it your ass or somebody else's?"

Connie blew away the smoke. "This is a very old movie. I really do not know anything."

"One more time," Green said. "And only one more time. Unless you don't like this place."

"She tried to beat up a couple of the regulars. Not in here. But *that's* why I banned her."

"I need the names."

"I've been thinking of moving to San Francisco, Mr. Green. These were confidences."

"I need the names, dear."

"These women would not kill anybody."

"You've been around too long to give me that shit." Green stood up.

"I have never in my life fingered anybody," Connie said.

"Especially if the corpse is white."

"I've been around too long for that shit too. Do whatever the hell you want, Noah."

"It's not just me, dear. Lieutenant Randazzo will be sending around folks who don't know Ben Webster from Gordon Liddy. They'll be wanting to talk to all your customers, and they'll be doing a lot of staring. Furthermore,"—Green leaned against the wall—"we both know that San Francisco is a very tacky town. People like you can't leave New York. Unless they're fixing to die. Well, maybe you have had it, Connie. Maybe you haven't got the balls for this city anymore."

Connie rose and looked down at Green. "Let me talk to them first. I'll call you tomorrow."

"And they'll be gone tomorrow."

"That's as far as I'll go, Noah. Take the chance or close me down."

"I'll get the names tomorrow, whatever they say to you?"

"Yup."

"If they've flown, Connie, don't bother coming down here tomorrow. And I'll have some other grief for you too."

"I should have known better," she said. "A Jew cop is like a mick cop is like a nigger cop is like a cop."

"I would hope so," Green said. "Isn't that what democracy is all about?"

Standing in front of Connie's, as Green was looking at a very large man running in place in an apartment across the street, something leapt on Green's back, landing so hard that his knees bent. It was growling, like an animal. Green's hand was on his gun as he turned to look into Merle Haggard's mocking eyes.

A whistle—a four-note lick from "White Line Fever" —and the dog loped to the tall man carrying a violin case. He was standing on the corner.

"You're going to lose him, Bama." Green walked over to the fiddler. "Fun is fun, but some citizen is going to slit his throat."

Bama laughed. "Nobody's that fast. Anyway, I only sic him on friends. Merle knows it's just fooling."

"What if one of your friends has a heart condition?"

"I apologize, Noah. It's just a down-home thing. Merle's sorry too."

The dog bared his teeth in what struck Green as a disgusting Uriah Heep smile.

"Bama, dogs have to be leashed. *Especially* him."

"It seems so hard, Noah, not to give Merle some running room. Actually, I usually take him out way early and way late—when hardly anybody's around. And when Emma takes him out, he's leashed for sure."

"She worries me," Green said, "staying so late in that store."

"Emma's got no fear, Noah. Nothing you can do with

somebody like that. I've tried. She's the kind of person, they start coming in with that H-bomb, she'll get on the roof to see what's going down. Worse than that, she goes on the subway all by herself at all hours. Well, I'm going down to see a guy about a gig. A rock club going country. Can't keep the truth from rising."

Waving, Bama walked off. Merle Haggard followed, then stopped for a moment and looked back at Green, who growled at him, softly.

In the light of a street lamp, earlier that evening, an exceedingly thin boy, with a cloud of red hair, was sitting on the stairs of a brownstone across the tree-lined street from the Ginsburg murder scene. As he went through a stack of newspapers, occasionally ripping out a story, the boy suddenly looked up—at Sam McKibbon. The gaze was so open and searching that McKibbon was uncomfortable.

"Cop, huh?" said the boy.

"How'd you come to that conclusion?"

"Well, you're on some kind of business, and you're not dressed like a meter reader or a painter, and anyway, it's too late for that."

McKibbon started to fill his pipe. "How do you know I'm on some kind of business?"

"Well," the boy said, "strangers come for dinner or after or whatever, they're kind of relaxed, you know. You got more than that on your mind. You see, I'm a journalist. I'm an intern at the *Villager*, and I practice making connections. Close observing, you know. Also," the boy's high, chirping voice was beginning to irritate McKibbon, "the odds are you're a cop because of what happened to Mrs. Ginsburg. One of you guys was here this morning, but I know that canvassing sometimes doesn't pay off until the second or third time."

"Did he talk to you, the guy who was here this morning?"

"No," the boy said. "I just saw him go up the stairs when I was on the way to school. I would have stopped, but I had an exam first period. It's my junior year. I can't mess up, you know. Then I went to the paper after school, and I just got back. I'm glad you came. I won't be missing anything."

"Okay,"—McKibbon sat down on the stairs, just above the boy—"did you know Mrs. Ginsburg?"

"Just to nod to. She was always in a hurry."

"You notice people coming in and out of her place?"

"Hardly ever. Not for a long time."

"Ever see her go out or come in *with* anybody?"

"No," said the boy. "Not even with her husband. Each of them came out alone, and each of them came back alone." The boy paused. "Well, I did see her with somebody last night. Actually, it was about one in the morning. They were down the street, arguing about something. I couldn't get the words. You see, they weren't loud, but you could sure tell they were arguing."

"That somebody—man or woman?"

The boy shook his head. "Sometimes it's hard to tell, especially down here. And anyway, they were in the doorway of that antique store." He pointed. "I could see Mrs. Ginsburg's back and just a little of—of the other person."

"Take your time," McKibbon said. "Give me all of whatever you saw."

"The other person was about her height," the boy said. "I couldn't see the face, and since they were talking so low, though hard, you know, I couldn't make out what that person sounded like."

"When did the other person leave?"

"Not long after I started watching. It walked toward Hudson Street."

"Wearing?"

"Some kind of coat," the boy frowned. "Gees, I thought I was better than this. I remember it was a coat and, and the collar was up. It was real cold."

"Man's coat? Woman's coat?"

"The kind that could be either. I'm embarrassed. I'm really embarrassed."

McKibbon smiled. "You weren't looking to remember, so you got no cause to be embarrassed about anything. Maybe if you think about it some more, when you're by yourself, you'll remember more. What were you doing out that late?"

The boy grinned. "It was a great night. They were shooting a movie way west in the Village. The gays were trying to shut it down. You must have read about it. Lots of cops. Some blood. Actually, a lot of blood. All kinds of things go on down here."

"Uh-huh. Your parents let you move around at all hours?"

"My mother. Single-parent home. We have a deal. I get good grades, don't smoke dope and don't turn gay, and I can do pretty much what I want."

McKibbon lit his pipe. "I'll give you my card. Anything comes to mind, give me a call. What's your name?"

"Adam. Adam Horowitz."

"Tell me, Adam," McKibbon said, "what's your impression of Mr. Ginsburg?"

"A creep," Adam Horowitz said. "Not that I know anything about him. I never even talked to him. But some people are just plain creeps. You can tell right away. You must have come across a lot of them."

"Why do you say that about him?"

"He always looks as if he's smelling something bad. It

must be coming from him. I mean, he's all dried up, you know. I've had teachers like him."

McKibbon moved up the stairs.

"Detective McKibbon,"—the boy took a long, narrow reporter's notebook from his jacket pocket—"would you say there's still a lot of prejudice in the Department?"

McKibbon looked at him somberly. "Anybody got brains in this Department, they're in real trouble, so that means people of color are in the most trouble of all. Now that, young man, is off the record."

"How about not for attribution?"

"Okay, provided it was told you by an unnamed blond detective with an Irish mug."

5 The cheerful din at Rafferty's was composed of *Kojak* on the huge color-television set over the bar, Frank Sinatra's "The Gal That Got Away"—allegedly a house favorite—on the jukebox, and the arm-waving patrons, intent only on rebutting each others' pronouncements.

The ancient bartender, his face permanently flushed, cigarette stuck to his lip, handed Green another club soda with a twist of lemon. The detective looked in the glass. "I said light on the ashes."

Chuckling, the old man took the cigarette out of his mouth and, leaning over to the detective to be heard, said, "Must be a lady coming. If you'd told me, I would have bought some clean glasses. None of my business, but how long have you been on those Carrie Nations. I remember nights, and they weren't too long ago, when you could kill a quart and nobody would know it but your mother and me."

"I wasn't quite in that league, Dennis," Green poked at the lemon. "But I was getting there. It isn't your business, but my old man was an oiler, and, lately, I began seeing him in the mirror. Okay?"

"Cripes," said the bartender, "I haven't heard that word for years. There was a captain in the Twenty-third who was one hell of an oiler. Before your time. I think Riordan broke in under him. Well, there used to be a chophouse a few doors from here. I was working there, and I'd bring the captain his lunch or his dinner. Didn't matter which. It was always the same. A big tureen. Inside, in case the inspector came by, home fries and tomato-and-onion salad. The main dish, in a grand teapot, a fifth of rye."

Green laughed. "I've done some variations on that."

"The captain retired," the bartender continued, "but he'd come back to the chophouse a couple of times a week. Out of the side of his mouth, he'd ask for the regular, tureen and all. He said the smell of the home fries gave the booze body, and the salad gave it class. You see, the poor man, he missed the con. Every cop needs a little adventure of his own on the side, wouldn't you say, Noah?"

The bartender looked past the detective and gave a slight bow to the redheaded woman who had materialized behind Green. The detective turned around.

"You're very punctual," Shannon Leahy said, her arms full of newspapers and magazines. "Most people aren't."

"You can set your watch by him," Dennis said. "And a teetotaler besides. He's almost too good to be true."

"You know what I'm going to give you for Christmas?" Green turned to the bartender. "Thirteen violations."

"Excuse *me.*" Dennis turned up the volume on the television set.

Green led the reporter to a booth in the back. She took out a cigarette and said, "I may have something that can be of use, but I'd like something in return."

Green kept looking at her.

"If this leads to anything," she went on, "I'd like it first."

"For all my talk," Green said, "I am not entirely inflexible in my attitude toward the press. Depending on the quality of the information. Which I have to hear before I can give you an answer."

Leahy lit the cigarette. "I know that's logical, but it could wind up with my being played for a schmuck."

"Women," said Green, frowning, "should not use the term schmuck in referring to themselves."

"How about *shmegegge?* The *shikseh shmegegge.* I broke in with a Jewish city editor of the old school. The all-gentiles-are-born-dumb school. Anyway, since everybody tells me you're a man of your word, here's what I got. Kathleen Ryan, as she was then, about six years ago, worked at the *Journal* on the copy desk. She was there a year or so. That you would have found out, and you probably have already. She left suddenly, without a word to anybody. Why she left might take you some time to find out.

"From what I hear—I wasn't there then," the reporter went on, "it was a bad scene in those years. Poisonous. The paper was crawling with factions. If you were in the wrong one, or worse yet, if you weren't in any, there was no way you could move up. Kathleen wanted to be a reporter. She wanted it desperately. She knew, from the copy she had to unscramble every day, that she was a hell of a lot more literate than most of the reporters, and she also knew that much of the time, they fucked up their stories."

Green winced.

She laughed. "My, you're an old-fashioned man. For a while, Kathleen used to come in with clips from the *Washington Post* and the *Wall Street Journal* and all kinds of places to show exactly how those stories had been screwed up. Better? Mishandled? Much better? But she wasn't exactly thanked for that.

"Anyway, she decided to get with the feminist faction which was tough, mean and, therefore, effective. There weren't enough blacks on the paper to frighten management, and no Puerto Ricans at all. But the feminists really got a network going. Secretaries copied internal correspondence, very high-level internal correspondence. Women in the finance department made the pay sheets available. Talk about unequal pay for the same job! Male reporters in our Washington office were making six, eight thousand a year more than the women reporters there."

"Your pleasure?" Dennis, having left the other bartender alone to deal with the standing drinkers, appeared at the booth.

"A brandy, please," Leahy said.

"The same,"—Green looked up at Dennis—"without comment."

"He said you were a teetotaler," the reporter smiled.

"He is a pathological liar. Go on," Green said.

"So, the paper, scared to death of a Title Seven suit, began to make reparations, and the feminist mafia got a lot of power over who got hired, and over promotions. For a loner, Kathleen tried awfully hard to be accepted by the sisterhood. But there was some shit she wouldn't eat. Sorry. Oh, what the hell, I don't tell you how to talk."

"I didn't say a fucking word," Green said.

"Good. The sisterhood, the mafia, would blacklist certain women because they were deficient, one way or another, in their commitment to liberation. If you flirted with men, or couldn't stand writing 'chairperson' or wondered aloud why there were still so few black males on the paper, you were in trouble when it came to those promotions."

"Fuck you! Fuck you! Who the hell are you to tell me how much I can drink?" The roar came from a beefy man of about fifty at the bar—to which he was holding on as if it might roll away. Green looked up, started to rise and then sat down again.

Without answering, Dennis reached below the bar, took out a baseball bat and said very distinctly, "Where you want it, on the left side, on the right side or right in your runny nose?"

The beefy man straightened up as best he could and, weaving, barely managed to get out the door. He was followed by a shower of change thrown by the bartender.

"Dennis is particular whose tips he accepts," Green said. "Go on."

"Kathleen was disgusted by the way the sisterhood was acting, and finally said so. That was it. Robin Feuerstein, she's still there, chief of the sisterhood's thought police, told Kathleen that she'd never get off the copy desk. And that she might not stay there very long either because her work was about to be examined for signs of sexism and other habitual crimes against women.

"In the middle of the city room,"—Leahy lit another cigarette—"Kathleen told Robin that she was an asshole —I'm just quoting, you understand—and an authoritarian cunt, and the most atrocious speller she'd ever seen. Kathleen then declared that the feminists at the paper had missed the whole point of feminism. That feminism is not solidarity with other feminists but solidarity with other women. And she walked out. For good."

Green looked at her and said sardonically, "And you think Robin, or one of the others, smarting all these years, finally rid the world of the traitor?"

"I think," Shannon Leahy said coldly, "that this may tell you something about the kind of person Kathleen was, and that may fit in with something else. Or it may not. And you are not welcome."

"Have another brandy," Green said, waving two fingers at Dennis. "That was reflexive. I have a habit of downgrading leads so I won't expect too much. Sometimes I'm wrong. But I was really just talking to myself. I do appreciate the information. And if it does lead to anything, I will try—our commander often insists on orchestrating these things himself—to let you know in front. You like jazz?"

Shannon Leahy looked at Green quizzically. "I must have missed the transition. Well, since you ask, I don't know much about it, but I usually like it when I hear it. Why?"

"Maybe some night we can hear some?" Green said to his brandy glass. "That is, if it's okay."

Shannon leaned back in the booth and stared at him. "Yeah, it's okay. I just didn't expect it. But what the hell, what's life without surprises?"

"Who else can I talk to at the paper," Green said, "about Kathleen's time there?"

"Let me think about that." She had put on her coat before Green could reach for it. "I'll let you know."

"After you clear it first with them?"

"Yeah. Anyway, I don't think there's any more to find out at the paper."

"One never knows, do one?" Green fingered a cigar in his pocket.

6 It was Sam McKibbon's theory that the most effective way to concentrate on a stalled case was to break concentration for a while. And his favorite way of doing that was to browse through Randazzo's file of homicides that had remained uncleared for months, sometimes years.

"I just like looking at the monster pictures," he had once told Green. "But you never know, sometimes a light gets turned on."

This morning, in the squad room, McKibbon had the file on his desk.

"When did he lose the eye?" Green said, looking over McKibbon's shoulder at one of the sheets. It had a profile and full-face shots of:

MARVIN WATSON— MURDER (KNIFE)
AKA PREACHER/M/B/ 28, *5'10"*, *145 lbs.*, black hair.
Last known address Greenhaven.
Subject is wanted for killing one Juan Torres
during a dispute. Notify 79 Pct. PIU.

"About seven years ago," said McKibbon, still looking at the picture. "Got his eye gouged out in one of them disputes. But no one saw a thing. The nerve of the mother, going around committing homicide with one eye."

Watson was black, bearded; had a thin face and a thick fold of flesh, with what looked like a slit in it, where his right eye would have been. The other eye was whole, clear and speculative.

"So maybe he wears dark glasses all the time," Green said.

"Yeah, but that's a trace in itself. But what the fuck am I talking about? He's still out there, with his lousy one eye. Some day we're going to have a perpetrator with two heads we can't find. Now that would be real embarrassing."

"I wonder,"—Green sat on the corner of the desk—"if you arrest a guy with two heads, do you have to read him his rights twice? You looking at the knife artists in particular today?"

"I stop a little longer on those sheets, yeah," McKibbon said.

"*Goddamn fucking imbeciles!*" The lyric tenor of Fortunato Randazzo filled the squad room. "We do this exactly the way I planned it."

"I'll be damned." McKibbon rose quickly. "Maybe there was something to it."

"To what?" Green asked.

"A snitch called the lieutenant a couple of hours ago. Said that maniac, Morales, didn't go back to Puerto Rico, like we thought, after he killed that jeweler. Said he's holed up in Chelsea. I didn't pay it much mind, we get so many tips on that fucking Morales. Anyway, the lieutenant sent down a team, including sharpshooters. But he wants a clean bust so he's directing the show from here."

"Why from here?"

"If the fuckhead *is* there, Randazzo's got a plan. He needs phones he can depend on."

"He's a maniac, all right, that Morales," Green said, as they hurried toward Randazzo's office. "Four homicides that we know about."

Standing at his desk, the lieutenant was yelling into a phone, "DON'T YOU EVER TRY TO BEGIN TO SECOND-GUESS ME LIKE THAT AGAIN! NOW, YOU'RE ABSOLUTELY SURE IT'S MORALES? You saw him clear as day when he looked out the window? But he didn't see you? Okay. I KNOW IT'S AN EASY SHOT, YOU ASSHOLE. I DON'T WANT TO HEAR THAT SHIT ABOUT ALL OF A SUDDEN YOU THINK MAYBE HE'S GOING FOR HIS GUN. NOW YOU LISTEN TO ME! I am now going to make the call to Morales and YOU ARE NOT GOING TO MOVE UNTIL I TELL YOU! UNDERSTAND? YOU DO NOT MOVE UNTIL YOU HEAR FROM ME. AND DON'T HANG UP BY MISTAKE!"

Randazzo carefully placed the telephone receiver on his desk, looked at Green and McKibbon and snapped, "Not a fucking word." He peered at a piece of paper on the desk, picked up another phone, dialed a number and, sounding hoarse and terribly hurried, whispered into the second phone, "Get out of there, the fucking cops just got the address."

The lieutenant hung up the second phone and bellowed into the first phone, which was still open, *"Now! Give them the signal!"*

Two minutes later, Randazzo, who had not let the open phone out of his hand, jubilantly nodded at what he was hearing. "Good. Very good. I can't wait to see those scumbags." And he put the phone down.

"The guys we had upstairs in the corridor,"—Randazzo turned to Green and McKibbon—"jumped Morales as soon as he ran out of the room after my call. We didn't need the backup guys. And the other two punks turned into water. There was only one set of balls among the three of them.

"It turned out beautiful." Randazzo clapped his hands

together. "Beautiful. Don't have to shoot up the place, don't have to go to any cops' funerals, don't have to cripple any bystanders. Well, I better shave for when the television comes. Another score for the *good* guineas. That's why I handle these press conferences personally, gentlemen. It's very important public relations for all us Americans with vowels at the end of our names. A, it shows we're not all wise guys. B, it shows we're smart. Smart as Jews." He looked at Green.

"At least," Green said.

"You'd be amazed," Randazzo said. "You'd be amazed how many people think guineas got olive oil for brains. I bet you guys did until you got into this precinct."

"Naw." McKibbon shook his head energetically. "When I was a kid, there was a little Italian shoemaker on the block who taught me that the Earth moves around the sun. Changed my whole life."

Randazzo grinned. "We got a minute to celebrate. Here—" He opened the bottom drawer of his desk and took out a quart of Johnny Walker Red and three paper cups.

"How come," said Green, "you don't drink grappa or some other tribute to your heritage?"

Randazzo looked at him. "You polish your mezuzah lately?"

They raised the paper cups, touched them together, drank the scotch and then, as best they could, dashed the paper cups to the ground.

"Okay," the lieutenant said, "back to the hard ones. The allegedly hard ones. What's going on with those two *bodega* killings? That was a nice old man, you know, the one who got it in the head. Used to come by and ask, very politely, when were we going to have a cop patrolling the neighborhood, like in the old days, the way the old Jews told him it used to be? What was I going to do, lie to him? So he stopped coming. Shit. You couldn't hold the black guy. What's his name? Stubblefield. So what *are* you doing?"

"I wanted to go back and canvass again," Green said, "but there's been no time. Maybe somebody else can take it."

"Come on,"—Randazzo pointed to a file on his desk— "we got three bodies over the weekend. No, you guys stay on it. You talk to Stubblefield again. He still could know something. That call you got from the snitch may not be all wrong, you know."

"I told you,"—Green fumbled for a cigar—"I haven't had a chance because of this Ginsburg case."

Grunting, the lieutenant took out a handkerchief and shined his spotless black shoes. "Speaking of which, what?"

"I'm going to go back and see that kid again," Sam McKibbon said. "He's the only one so far who saw her with anybody that night."

Green took another paper cup, poured more scotch into it and turned to the lieutenant. "I'm looking into the lesbian angle. And I'm keeping company with the professor."

"You know something?" Randazzo said. "I'm glad I don't have any kids. I couldn't take it if they turned queer. I could not take it. I think I'd kill them. Or myself. No, better them so they wouldn't infect anybody else.

"Listen,"—Randazzo turned to Green—"lean on the husband. He's got to know more than he told us. But be nice. We don't want to scare him into getting a lawyer. Be nice. Until you got him by the balls."

Green was to meet Ginsburg in Washington Square Park, near the fountain. The squad room was the last place in the world for a conversation with the professor.

At this point. Leaning against a wall of the arch, Green surveyed the assorted citizens taking the winter sun. A few mothers and children, scarecrows in the form of winos, students from NYU and snapshots from his official past.

Out of the first ten people he checked out lounging around the fountain, for instance, Green saw six familiar masks. He tried to reconstruct what he could remember of their careers. Charges, not dispositions. Two second-degree assaults, two or three menacings *(shit, no point counting misdemeanors)*, one manslaughter second degree, two second-degree criminal possessions of stolen property, at least four criminal possessions of controlled substances in varying degrees, a bunch of third-degree criminal sales of marijuana and one first-degree rape. There was more, but he couldn't sort it out. *Oh, yeah, promoting a sexual performance by a child. His eight-year-old stepdaughter. Fucker shaved his mustache.*

There they all were: thin and fat, scarred and sleek, with maggots for eyes.

Green had no idea how much time each had served for his accomplishments because he had little remembrance of the lesser charges each had been gifted with on plea-bargain day. Between the supercilious assistant DAs and the gutless judges, it was a wonder they had served any time at all.

If he were a praying man, Green smiled as the remedy entered him, he would ask, beseech, bang his head against the Wailing Wall, that God should bring a pitiless plague of rapes, aggravated sexual abuse and muggings of the wives and mothers and sisters and daughters, especially the daughters, of one out of every six assistant DAs and judges up through the appellate division to the very Court of Appeals itself. One of the ambulatory mug shots at the fountain recognized Green and, with a smile enhanced by rotting teeth, gave him the finger. If they were dogs—the detective put his left hand on the upper part of his right arm, simultaneously drawing up his right forearm to return the greeting—they would have been put to sleep a long time ago.

As Green looked toward University Place for a sign of Ginsburg, another familiar felon materialized beside the detective, but so silently and swiftly that Green was annoyed at being startled. A large man of indeterminate age, black, muscular, a small gold earring in his right ear, a face that looked as if it had been stepped on when he was born. "You really on the shit list, Captain," he said in a soft, gurgling voice, "scavenging down here. What happened? Gun go off by accident, hee, hee?"

Green automatically felt for his gun, and the black man laughed. "You know me better than that, Captain. Had I wished, I would have cut your head off before you even blinked. But I did not want to. When I take you, it's gonna be for bread. The working class can't afford fun."

"Barney," the detective asked, "what was the last book you read?"

"What the fuck you want to know that for?" said Barney, annoyed at being surprised.

"I'm doing a survey for the lieutenant. Making up a Christmas list for those folks we figure we'll be sending away next year and we want to give them something to take with them."

"Ask your mama, motherfucker."

Green looked up at the sky, concentrated and said:

They rung my bell to ask me
Could I recommend a maid.
I said, yes, your mama.

Barney roared. "Hot dog! I forgot you knew Langston.

That man would talk with anybody. A kind, kind man he was. I'd say, 'Mr. Hughes, I can't work on my poems because the only thing I can think of is how hungry I am.' And he'd give me some bread. Every time, he'd give me some bread."

"And you'd give it to the junkman."

"Sure. I was doing what you folks wanted me to do."

"You misread the ticket," Green said. "Yours said overdose. I sure was sorry when you kicked it. At least there was a limit to what you could do when shit was all you thought about."

"I come back," Barney grinned, "just to hear you say that. Well, enough funnin'. They switch you to narcotics?"

"Nope," Green said, "I'm still mostly specializing in corpses. Not the walking dead, with dirt in all their holes, like you and that Arthur keep fucking over."

"I don't know any Arthur," Barney said. "All rightee, Captain. As always, it has been enchanting talking to you. Your color ain't good though. You look like something's eating at you. What do they say? Yeah, *bon appetit* whatever you are inside the captain. Hey, maybe it's cancer. Yeah, I bet you it is cancer. I will make a contribution in your name. And I'll visit your grave. Ain't nobody else gonna do it. Hee, hee." And Barney loped away as Burton Ginsburg came near.

"I didn't want to interrupt the conversation," Burton Ginsburg said, walking over to the detective. "I thought he might be an informant."

"No," Green said. "He's a sociology professor at Yale, doing field research. Let's sit over there."

Ginsburg took the *New York Times* out of a large leather envelope, found the business section, laid it on the bench and sat on it.

The detective watched three neatly dressed black

men, in their late teens and early twenties, move swiftly and purposefully through the circle around the fountain. Recognizing none of them, Green frowned, but when one tried briefly, and successfully, to catch Barney's eye, Green nodded to himself.

"I appreciate your coming, professor," the detective said.

"Do you have any leads?" The professor was as self-possessed as ever.

"We're still gathering information. You didn't tell us your wife was a lesbian."

"I don't know anything about that," Ginsburg said evenly. "Whatever she did outside the house, I know nothing about."

"You had no idea, no suspicion?"

Ginsburg folded his hands. "It is no longer all that unusual to have that kind of secret in a marriage. And Kathleen, when she wanted to be, was extraordinarily discreet. Indeed, she was the most private person I have ever known."

Green took out a cigar. "You don't mind in the open air?"

"I do. The air is polluted enough as it is."

"Can I chew on it?" Green, to his regret, had raised his voice.

"I would recommend zwieback instead, but go ahead."

Green broke the cigar in half and threw it away. "You told me why you stayed together. Would you mind telling me why and how you got married?"

"I was lonely. I had never married before. I am not particularly forthcoming by temperament. I never learned how to—as the young say nowadays—make the moves. But I had always been self-sufficient. Yet, increasingly, I very much wanted someone to talk to at night.

I wanted to hear a voice besides my own. I had actually taken to talking to myself in the house, and felt very foolish about that. But when I did not speak aloud, the silence could become unbearable."

Ginsburg rubbed his forehead. "I would often leave the house and walk where there were people, just to hear other voices. But that is not very satisfactory. Then I met Kathleen. She was intelligent, extremely articulate and, to be sure, rather abrasive. But I always liked a sharp argument. And I was sexually attracted. But I could do without that. I had always been doing without that."

"And she? Why did she marry you?"

"I don't know. I often asked myself that."

"You never asked *her?*"

"Seldom. Whenever I did, she would laugh. Not unpleasantly."

Green watched Barney leaving the park with, now, six young men in his retinue. "How did you meet?"

"At Cooper Union Hall. I was giving a lecture on Dickens, and she came up afterward to disagree. Quite savagely. But intriguingly."

"What about?"

"My view is that Dickens was the equal of the nineteenth-century Russians—actually superior in breadth and detail, since he knew much more about all kinds of people than Dostoevski or Tolstoy. And he was also far, far more truly humane—"

"And she?"

"Kathleen said that Dickens was embarrassingly sentimental, and at best a caricaturist. And caricature is hardly high art. She also said that only men really enjoyed Dickens because of their preference for the simplistic."

"So you got married?"

"Not too long after." The professor smiled faintly.

"There was so much to talk about. I mean, to disagree about. I was delighted. At first. And even after the combat became incessantly nasty, even after the end of any sexual relations between us, I looked forward to coming home. We did, you see, communicate."

"What happened to end the sexual relations?" Green looked at the trees.

"That seems a rather voyeuristic line of questioning," Ginsburg said without asperity. "All right. I had become impotent. And it was too humiliating, after a while, to keep trying."

"There are other things you could have done."

"Kathleen did not want to do them."

"I'll get off this in a minute," Green said, "but you must have missed the touching, the holding."

"There had never been much of that. Look, as you know, I do not have to answer those questions I do not choose to. Obviously, I do want to be of help, but I can't see how—"

"If I may go back, you never knew she was a lesbian?"

Ginsburg said coldly, "I will repeat. She never told me."

"What if she had?"

"If she had wished to stay," Ginsburg said, "and if she had kept that part of her life outside of the house, I could have borne it. Better than if she had found a male lover. You understand?"

"Sure," Green said. "Now that you know, could she have married you to have a front? Wasn't she the kind of woman who would have been more comfortable appearing straight?"

"As I told you, she was a very private woman, but she did not give a damn what anybody thought about anything she did. She was private for other reasons, and don't ask me what they were, because I don't know. Do you understand the distinction I am making? She did not want people to assume they knew her, but whatever they thought they knew about her, the only assessment of her that mattered was her own."

"Would you have believed it possible that she was a lesbian?" Green asked.

"I believe anything is possible. I am very widely read, if not widely experienced."

Green leaned back on the bench. "What did she tell you about her time at the *Journal?*"

The professor frowned. "I didn't know she had worked there. She told me very little about her previous life. Her father had been a high-school teacher in Ohio, mathematics. She had gone to Earlham College, come to New York and free-lanced—as she had been doing during our marriage."

"That's all?"

"Just about. She liked to talk about ideas mainly, not people, including herself. I'm very much the same way."

Green recognized another mug shot coming toward them. "Oh, one more thing. How many keys were there to your home?"

"Two. Mine and Kathleen's."

"Are you absolutely certain no one else had a key?"

"I know I never gave one to anybody, and I would be astonished if Kathleen had. I never saw the slightest indication that she had. I'm home every night, and I pop in at various times during the day because NYU is quite near."

"Of course, somebody could have knocked on the door that night, and she let him in. Or her. Or whomever."

"It's possible," said Ginsburg, clearly thinking that it was not. He put up his collar against the late-afternoon cold. "But it's not like Kathleen. She was deathly afraid of unexpected knocks at the door. About the only thing she was afraid of."

"What if it was a knock she expected?"

"I wouldn't know anything about that. But I do not think it at all likely. Not at that time of night. Not in our house."

Ginsburg rose. "We haven't gotten very far, have we?"

Green also got up. "An inch here, half an inch there—you fall back two inches another place and then, out of nowhere, somebody calls you and tells you everything you want to know."

"You are putting me on, Mr. Green."

"Not exactly, professor."

"Tell me, you are quite certain Kathleen was a lesbian?"

"I wish I hadn't had to tell you. And I wouldn't have, if I'd had any doubts."

"Well," Ginsburg said, "I guess it wasn't all my fault, then. I suppose I should thank you."

7 Bone-thin, the lightest shade of beige, so tall his head floated over the throng around the fountain as he jogged at high noon the next day. A spear of black, gray and white, and blue sneakers. His eyes catching every little thing, the points of his thin, elegant mustache looking like antennae, Arthur circled the park effortlessly, again and again.

"All the fucker ever do is run," one of Barney's junior executives observed amiably.

"No, man," said his companion, who had the look of an upright turtle. "He be with Barney a lot."

"But what's he *do?*"

"You know what Barney say, 'What I don't tell you, you don't ask about, if you want to stay this side of the earth.'"

"Hmph. You ever talk to him, that Arthur?"

"Once," said the turtle. "He ask me to go somewhere, and he give me a package, and he look at me, real close so I had to look at him, right in his eyes, 'cause that's all was in front of my eyes, and he say, 'Don't mess up, Russell. 'Cause if you mess up, I'm gonna have to cut off your pecker.' And he smile, like he could see himself doing it. Shit, I wish I'd been somewhere else that day."

"Why? You still got your thing."

"I dream about it, man. I see his eyes. Through the window. Or in the keyhole. I'm in a bed in this dream, and I see his eyes. Not the face. Could be anybody's face. But the eyes are his. And they want me. They want to do it to me. They full of want, those eyes. Never saw nothing so hungry. Gonna bite off my pecker."

"You sure he ain't a faggot?"

"I ain't even sure he's human."

Across the park, Arthur gracefully slackened his pace until he stopped in front of a bench where Barney sat, his face thrown back, smiling in the wintry sun.

"Earl wants a deal," Arthur said in a clipped West Indian rhythm. "The man with steel in his head and also Earl's own brother, mind you, they're turning."

"How does he know?" Barney addressed the sun.

Arthur smiled. "A friend. An expensive friend. What is called a mole. In the United States Attorney's office."

"Shee-it." Barney straightened up, looked at Arthur and grinned. "The mole go with the deal?"

"I think that is a separate matter," Arthur said. "It should be a separate matter."

"I know. Just funnin'. Do we get it all? All the coke on hand, all the coke in the pipeline and the connections for all the coke after that?"

"All. Earl knows he will take a bath, but he needs a stake, fast. He is going far, far away. He does not want to go to prison under any circumstances."

"How much you figure this going to cost us?" Barney yawned.

"We did not talk numbers. That is for you. But I figure we can handle it ourselves."

"The Feds must be tailing him."

"Not yet." Arthur frowned at a smudge on one of his sneakers. "The mole in the United States Attorney's office says not yet. They are not ready yet. But they will start very soon. That's why Earl wants to be gone instantly."

"All rightee," Barney said. "Bring Earl to the Blimpie's on Eleventh Street. Like around seven. Alone."

"Earl is a gourmet cook, you know," Arthur said without expression.

"Fuck him. Cheap place, cheaper deal. You been looking after that Whipple?"

"Yes, he is all by himself. He does not deal drugs. He is not in our way."

Barney stretched. "Anything else?"

Arthur smiled. "I hear the police found Anthony. But they are disappointed in having only the middle of him. They anxiously await the rest. Especially the head."

Barney chuckled. "If we still had them, we could at least send them Anthony's ears. That rotten snitch. After all I did for him."

The beige man nodded judiciously. "He was suicidal, that Anthony. We merely assisted him in getting it over with. We were a blessing to him. He could not fit anywhere at all in this life. Well, I have not done all my miles yet." And Barney's general manager, erect and serene, jogged away.

Late that night, west of Washington Square, not far from the river, Emma, standing over the bed, looked into the fiddler's face.

He sleeps like a child; he always sleeps like a child. And when the gin is in him—God, he drinks that stuff like water—he sleeps like a dead child. But he always wakes clear. Even when he's drunk, you can't tell he is. Except I can tell. He starts talking about his daddy. Glad I never met that man. Damn cracker.

There was a cough, a low growl, outside the door.

"Merle Haggard," Emma whispered at the growl, "one day soon I am going to poison you. But you're so mean, the poison will run right out."

I can't get over it. Me loving someone so white. Bama could almost be an albino. I don't even like that fiddle.

Doesn't say nothin' to me. He does. Good Lord, he does. Yes, indeed. Time for a child, Alabama.

Pull down your window, lock up your door,
Lock up on your window, lock up on your door,
I got ways like the devil, I'm slipping on the floor.

Yes, it's time for a child. Coming up to thirty-two. Coming up fast. Merle Haggard, you're going to be good and gone when that child comes. Wouldn't trust you a minute.

There was a scratching at the door.

That is no dog. That is a spirit. A fiend. Damn you, Merle Haggard. Time for a child. You hear me, Alabama?

Emma took off her robe, slipped into the bed, kissed the fiddler in the ear and on the eyes. His breathing did not change. Outside the window, someone on the street was whistling, and inside, hoarse, furious barking at the whistler.

"Heeey,"—Bama stirred—"what time is it?"

"Thank you, dear Merle Haggard," Emma whispered.

"Well, it doesn't matter." Bama turned and put his arms around her. "Devil comes up and asks me, 'What in the whole world do you want the most?' And I tell the devil, 'I already got it, you damn fool.' "

"What if he says,"—Emma snuggled against him—" 'Give up that woman and you'll be the best fiddle player there ever was, or ever will be.' "

Bama laughed. "No, Devil, I'm pretty damn good as it is, and being the best—Hell, it ain't worth not having my fiddling hand where it is now."

"Bama," she said, "it's time for a child."

"I been meaning to say the very same thing. But why just say it?"

Merle Haggard stared steadily at the bacon in the pan on the stove.

"No, sir, no good for you," Emma said. "On the other hand—" She cheerfully threw him a half-dozen strips.

"Looks like I'm going to be doing some lead singing with the band," Bama said from the kitchen table.

"About time. How come?"

"Johnny's going back down to West Virginia for a while. He's all broke up."

"They finally busted up, huh?" Emma poured the coffee. "About time for that too."

"She skipped." Bama was looking out the window. "He came home yesterday morning, and she'd cleared out. He knows whose bed she's gone to, but he says you can't force someone to stay with you that don't want to. There's a weakness in Johnny. That's what's wrong with his singing too. He's too damn sweet. You don't hear Merle being sweet. I mean the other Merle."

"What would you have done if you were Johnny?"

"Killed them both." He smiled at her. "I wouldn't want *her* no more, and I couldn't let him be taking what was mine."

"I'll keep that in mind." Emma threw the dog more bacon.

"Aw,"—Bama smiled all the way—"no way in this world that can happen to us. Anyway, wouldn't you do the same?"

Emma put her hand on her chin and looked at Merle Haggard without seeing him. "No," she said. "I'd get some lye and take off her face, and I'd cut off your repeater pistol, and I'd think of both of you every day with such satisfaction that it wouldn't matter what they did to me."

Bama got up and put an arm around her waist. "Now that's what I call true love," he said into her hair.

Around midnight, hours before, Crocker Whipple, hunched over, immersed in some inner dialogue, was rustling along—looking so fragile that the fierce, cold wind might have seized and lifted him high above Washington Square Park had he not sat down on a bench. Empty. Under the globes of light, it was all empty. He closed his eyes and opened them, to see suddenly two tall, thin, young blacks flowing toward him. They stopped directly in front of him.

One of them, wearing a black raincoat, said, "Gonna make it easy for you. Give me your money and you can keep your face." From his sleeve he drew a knife with a six-inch blade and touched it to Whipple's cheek.

"Fuck off, gentlemen," Whipple smiled. "I'm waiting for Barney."

The two teenagers looked at each other. "What you want with Barney?" asked the boy with the knife.

"I'm going to give him a blow job." Whipple's smile grew broader. "I can fit you two in if you make it snappy."

"Shee-it," said the other, who had no coat but was snug in a thick wool sweater. "I remember you. You the meat man."

"What do you upstanding citizens do for a living?" Whipple leaned back on the bench. "Let's see, you're in that special program, tutoring your little brothers and sisters in reading. No, that's not it. Wait a minute. You bring in hot lunches to the old folks and take them out for walks, and you go with them when they cash their Social Security checks so they don't get ripped off by the animals. No, that's not it either. I got it! You deal shit. Whatever kind of shit you can get hold of. There it is, gentlemen, you sell your kind of pleasure, I sell mine."

"Little boys!" The young man in the raincoat bent over and made as if he were throwing up. "Little boys, that's what you sell."

"Little boys,"—Whipple nodded agreeably—"big boys, black boys, yellow and white boys. Women too, women doing it all kinds of ways. It would tear your balls out with envy to watch women doing it to each other. What they can do with their fingers! Whoo-ee! I tell you, gentlemen, it's like watching a virtuoso guitarist. Acoustic guitarist, if you know what that means. And what some of those women can do with their big toes! My, my. No question about it. No man in this world can do it to a woman like another woman can do it to a woman. But that's only natural, right? They *know*."

"You are something that come up with the puke," said the young man in the black raincoat.

"Shit," his companion said, "he be something to be stepped on good."

"I feel like carving," said the black raincoat. "Gonna cut a big C in your face. For cunt, you know." The knife broke Whipple's skin under his right eye.

Impassive, Whipple said softly, "Barney gonna take your hand, break off all the fingers, one by one, and stick them up your ass, one by one."

The knife disappeared into the black youngster's sleeve. His companion spit close to, but not touching, Whipple's shoes. And they walked off.

Whipple remained on the bench, pulling a pocket radio from his corduroy jacket, fiddling around until he found a classical music station, and then closed his eyes again. One of them, anyway. "Ah, Pavarotti," Whipple murmured, "what big toes you must have."

Ten minutes later, Barney eased down beside Whipple.

"Pretty," Barney said. "But it don't move. Cat got no time. Band got no time. You want singing, you listen to Sarah Vaughan with a rhythm section; she cut that wop all to pieces."

Whipple fingered the slight cut below his right eye. "Two of your gracious younger associates have been by." He turned to Barney. "I had to tell them I was meeting you or I'd be in the emergency room at Saint Vincent's right now, with one of those good sisters asking the doctor what that C in the middle of my face is for."

Barney laughed. "My boys, they always practicing their alphabets 'cause they want to get ahead."

"I thought they had more profitable things to do."

"When they on their own time," Barney said, "I let them fun a little. You tell them what we're meeting about?"

"I wouldn't dream of doing that."

Barney laid a huge hand on Whipple's shoulder. "Smart little faggot. I don't want them knowing nothing but what they got to know. I got a lot of corporations, each one separate from the other, so if one goes bust, I'm still in business. Now, I need a high-class whore. White. Young. No more than twenty. One who does it part-time. The customer likes to fall in love, you know, hee, hee. One of them actresses you got."

Whipple nodded. "Prices are up, Barney."

"So are mine." Barney shifted his bulk to get a better view of the street. "Pretty soon, *all* the prices gonna be mine. Pretty soon, I ain't gonna need you at all."

"Stocking up, huh?"

"I'm getting there, man. An outside supplier don't make no sense. Especially with what I've got in mind, which I ain't telling you."

"A monopoly of all the private parts for sale in the city?" Whipple smiled.

"Just Manhattan. I ain't greedy. In the meantime, I also need a woman. A woman for a woman. Don't matter what color. This is an equal opportunity cunt licker. But clean. The woman got to be clean. No coke. No big boozer. Muggles are okay."

"Muggles?" Whipple giggled. "How quaint you do sound sometimes. You're a lot older than you look."

"I got no age," Barney growled. "Hey, you do much wholesale besides me? I know you do a lot of your own retail."

"No, you're my only corporate client. I'm no competition."

"Maybe I won't eat you up, hee, hee, when the time comes. I kind of like you, fag though you be. You a self-starter; you run your own little thing. Yeah, I like that, long as you don't get big eyes. Now, I got an old fruit who doesn't want to get bruised, dig? You can guarantee that?"

"Sure," Whipple said. "Can you guarantee *him?*"

"You got a point. It will be made clear. And, let's see, someone wants a boy, but I don't deal in that. And I don't make no referrals in that neither. You know, that's the one thing bothers me about you. Dealing in them boys."

Whipple lit a cigarette. "It's not what it looks like, Barney. A lot of those boys go looking for men. They get things they don't get at home, when they were home."

"That's what I mean, damn it!" Barney had raised his voice, and looked around.

"No, no. I'm talking about affection. I've seen boys really find a home, weird though it seems to you, where somebody cares about them. Like one guy, he makes the boy living with him go to school regularly. Gives him five dollars every morning, but only if the boy promises he's going to school. And the guy checks the school every once in a while on the phone, says he's an uncle."

"Shee-it," Barney said. "What good is school going to do the little pervert? He's already learned enough to mess him up forever. It's bad enough they want to fuck those boys, but don't tell me they turn into their mamas when they ain't going up their asses."

"There's good in that too, Barney. Children have sexuality, a lot of it. Freud himself said that children—"

"Fuck Freud. There's a guy that was on coke all the time, and people act like he knew what he was saying. No, man, that is disgusting, climbing all over little boys." Barney stared at Whipple. "You do it yourself?"

Whipple smiled. "You tell me what you do, and I'll tell you what I do."

Barney guffawed. "You ashamed?"

Whipple reddened. "Not at all. Not at all. Yes, I've done it with boys. What do you do, Barney?"

"Nothin'. Not one thing. I keep all my energy for myself. I don't get hung up on anybody—for one second. That's why my head is always so clear. That's why I don't get distracted. Ain't nobody gets to me."

"So you masturbate?"

Barney was shocked. "God damn, a man don't masturbate. Boys masturbate."

Crocker looked at Barney with new interest. "Then you really don't do anything?"

"Well, let me put it this way. I do a whole lot of mind-fucking. I get right inside people's heads and I fuck them over. And over and over. That's how I get off, man."

"Literally?"

"Sometimes," Barney smiled. "Sometimes, when I really screw somebody real bad, somebody who thought sure he was screwing me, I get to feel nice and wet."

Whipple shivered slightly. "It's getting too cold, Barney. You got the addresses and times?"

Barney gave him a slip of paper. "Remember who these clients belong to."

"I'd sooner forget my own name," Whipple said as he rose from the bench.

"Well, little faggot," said Barney, "have a nice day."

8 In the squad room the next morning, McKibbon, reaming out his pipe, asked his partner,
"You think Stubblefield's skipped?"

"Looks like it," Green said. "Super hasn't
seen him. He's not been at work. I call him at home three
in the morning, three in the afternoon, odd hours in
between. Nothing."

"And your cuchifrito snitch?"

"Domingo's gone back to the island for a couple of
weeks," Green said. "There's elections coming up."

"The dead will walk again. Listen, if Stubblefield has
skipped, Domingo may have been right in the first place.
The guy's on parole. Why else would he disappear if he
hadn't done that grocery job?"

Green shook his head. "I just don't believe it. That guy
was not jiving me. There's something very peculiar
about that *bodega* case, but there's no fucking time to
find out what. Well, I got to go see those lesbos before
they change their minds. They've been out of town, so
Connie says, but they just called in."

"Fix your tie." McKibbon looked at him. "Maybe you
can change your luck."

"My luck ain't ever going to be that bad," Green said.

An hour later, in the sunny Soho apartment of the
lesbians whom Kathleen Ginsburg had allegedly tried to
assault, Green felt sad. A cheerful expanse of white walls,
brightly colored tapestries, fresh flowers, everything so

clean. The younger woman, in her early twenties, slender, long, straight, light brown hair, large round glasses. Crisp. Sexy-crisp. The way one of Noah's junior-high-school teachers had looked. What a waste.

The other lesbian, taller, late twenties, slightly heavier, her dark hair cut short, also was attractive. On the street, Green would not have made her for a dyke. Such a nice ass. God, what a waste.

Meg, the older woman, was the talker. Yes, each of them had had an experience with Kathleen Ginsburg, although they had not known her last name. On first impression, she had seemed quite intelligent, with a lot of ideas about a lot of things. Strong ideas. Meg had met Kathleen at Connie's, and a long conversation had led to a subsequent dinner. At Meg's apartment. But Kathleen had wanted more than dinner and conversation, and became abusive when Meg told her there was no dessert.

"She tried to beat you up?" Green asked.

"I would say that was one of her intentions," Meg said evenly, "but I can handle myself very well. She *was* surprisingly strong, but too eager. I kicked her out the door. I mean that literally. Then I told her I would kick her down the stairs if she dallied, and she did not. Pretty much the same thing happened to Linda,"—she looked at the woman with the large round glasses—"a couple of weeks later."

"You hadn't told Linda about it?" Green was trying to read the titles on the bookshelf.

"We didn't know each other then."

"How did *you* handle her?" Green turned to Linda, who unexpectedly smiled.

"Martial arts," Linda said brightly. "It's always very effective."

"You've had to beat off a lot of women?" Green was

annoyed with himself for being interested beyond the call of duty.

"I never said that." Linda lit a cigarette. "She's the only *woman* I've had to do that with."

"Did either of you ever see Kathleen again?" the detective asked.

"Once or twice at Connie's," Meg said. "We ignored her. Now, we've spoken to you because Connie asked us to. If we are not suspects, and I can't imagine how we could be, would you please leave?"

"Could I impose on you for some tea?" Green remained seated. "With lemon. Just a few more questions."

The kitchen was at one end of the large, main living and sleeping room. Meg put on the water and watched Green.

"Those conversations each of you had with her," the detective continued. "What were some of those strong ideas she had?"

"Oh,"—Linda adjusted her glasses—"it's hard to remember specifics after all this time. One remembers the passion of the talk more than what it was about. She didn't much like male gays. I remember that. Kept calling them devious. And sex-ridden, which made them all the more devious."

"She said," Meg cut in, "that the difference between us and them, and it was a fundamentally revealing difference, was that we didn't do it in toilets. And we didn't go after little girls. She really had a thing about this so-called boy love. Not that I disagree with her. The rest, as I remember, had to do with books and music. You wouldn't be interested in that."

"I can barely get through the *Daily News*," Green said.

Meg brought him a cup of tea. "Do you have anything else?" she said.

Green took a few sips and rose. "Something may occur to me, in which case I'd greatly appreciate a bit more of your time. Tell me," he said to Meg, "what would you have done if Kathleen, rather surprisingly strong as she was, had persisted that night? If she had not left?"

"What do you want me to say?" Meg said coolly. "That I would have gotten a knife and plunged it into her back? She was just a pain in the ass, Mr. Green. You just get rid of a pain in the ass. I am also a lot stronger than I look. Kicking her downstairs would have been sufficient."

"Then I guess," Green said, "she was more than a pain in the ass to somebody else."

"Precisely," Meg nodded. "That should be a productive line of inquiry."

"I'm most grateful. And you," Green asked Linda, "what would you have done if she had kept coming after you?"

Linda laughed. "You weren't there. It took only a few seconds. And after that, she hadn't the slightest desire to keep coming after me. Or rather, the slightest ability. Would you like me to show you?"

Green longed for her waist, and smiled. "Another time, my dear."

Now that his hair was all white and he was a civilian, Jeremiah Riordan had let it grow fuller. Indeed, it billowed over his collar, a condition he never would have permitted in his men when he was commander of the First Homicide Squad in the lower precincts of Manhattan. In his fifth year of retirement, Riordan's cheeks and nose were rosy, his light blue eyes as cold as ever.

In his fourth-floor walk-up in Chelsea, near the river, Riordan sat in the kitchen, opposite the black detective who, in hope of illumination, had been filling him in on the case. Pouring himself another cup of tea, Riordan splashed some Gordon's gin in the cup. Sam McKibbon's cup was still full.

"Since it's the Hebrew's case, and he doesn't know you're here," Riordan said, "I can't very well go down and look at the crime scene." His voice was low, almost a whisper. It was Riordan's habitual way of talking for, as he used to tell the men in his command, "Walls have ears, and not all of them were put in there by us."

"It's all cold now," McKibbon said. "What would be the point? You've seen the photographs; you've got the crime-lab reports."

"Oh, death always leaves something behind, even after our crime-scene boys have departed with all their crumbs of revelation. I mean no mysticism, Sam. I cannot walk into a room at random and tell you that death has been there. But when I know it has visited, violently, I respond differently; I see differently."

"I can get you in," McKibbon said. "When the professor is in class."

"No, I would only go if the Hebrew knew. He caught the case. It is not for me to secretly intrude." Riordan smiled. "And you can't tell him you came to me, because he feels I tried to block him in the Department, right?"

"Yup," McKibbon said.

"Because he is Jewish?" Riordan smiled again.

"Yup."

Riordan took some more of the strong tea. "He is not incorrect. With very rare exceptions, Hebrews are not suited for police work. Most have a terrible case of hubris. It comes from that religion of theirs, the chief tenet of which is not only that they are the chosen but that they are so much smarter than anybody else. You've heard that insulting phrase of theirs, *goyisher kop?* And they'll say it where you can hear it, knowing that dumb as you are—not being one of them—you have the meaning anyway."

"It's a joke," McKibbon said.

"Have you any doubt at all that they believe it, with every part of them, including their circumcised cocks? 'We're not only smarter than you, we're cleaner, and we're cleaner because we're smarter.'"

"You believe Noah is smarter than you?"

Riordan hooted. "Nobody is, lad, as you well know."

"Then why let that *goyisher kop* stuff get to you?"

"Shall I call you *nigger* from now on, boy?"

McKibbon had some gin.

"It is the arrogance," the old man went on. "They are always challenging you and mocking you with their arrogance. The more persecuted they have been through the centuries, the more arrogant they become for having survived and prospered yet again."

"You blocked Noah because his parents or his grandparents didn't get wiped out in some pogrom?"

"Let me explain it to you then." Riordan leaned back in the kitchen chair and addressed the ceiling. "Police work is team work. And there can be no true team work without a certain humility that will allow you to look to others to make up for your failures of perception. Or will. Or faith. You catch me? But Hebrews are so certain of their superiority that they never really confide in anyone not of their religion. So much for having Hebrews on your team."

"But Noah—"

"Let me finish. This is not to say that Hebrews work well with each other either. I have seen that. Each going his own self-exalted way. For both these reasons, too many Hebrews in any one place create rancor, both among themselves and among everyone else. And if one of them is placed in a command post, why, there can be no leadership because there is no trust. The Hebrew will not trust in the competency of anyone but himself. And the men will not trust the Hebrew's capacity to give them some credit for even minimal intelligence."

Riordan poured the rest of the gin into the teacup. "And if there are other Hebrews among those under him, each will connive to get the job for himself. It is their way. They are a poisonous lot, Sam. What I did against him, I did for the Department. Not that Randazzo has so radiant a mind, but he knows how to command loyalty, and how to give loyalty, does he not?"

"Yeah," McKibbon said. "In his way. But you got Noah wrong. He doesn't fit your description of the prototypical Jew. Noah and I trust each other. And he's as much a part of the team as I am, whatever that may mean."

"Ah, lad, you haven't seen as much of them and as many of them as I. There are Hebrews so skilled at disguising their true natures that they can even get between the legs of good Christian girls."

"Oh come on, Lieutenant." McKibbon reached for the bottle of Gordon's. He began to laugh. "You mean, if us niggers don't get inside those white Christian legs first."

"Ah, Sam,"—Riordan took another bottle of gin from a carton under the kitchen table—"that was not worthy of you. But you will learn. You will learn why they have been hated through the ages, and why, if you could look into their frantic souls, they hate themselves. Now, she was lying on her right side. What was on her face?"

"The last surprise." McKibbon took out his tobacco pouch.

"Fright?"

"No, she got it from the back."

"She may have been running away."

"No, there was no fear there. But you've looked at the photographs."

"I want to know what *you* saw," said the old man.

"Well, it seemed to me—but how the hell can you be sure?—that just before the shock, almost wiped out by it, there had been a kind of disgust."

"Or gas," Riordan laughed dryly. "Still, you have a careful eye. Let us say disgust, then. It may connect later. The man, if it was a man, that the boy saw?"

"Hebrew boy. Can we trust him?" McKibbon smiled.

"Why not? There's nothing in it for him that we know about. That person he saw was about the woman's height. And the departed was—"

"Five-four," McKibbon said.

"The professor is how tall?" Riordan was writing on a laundry bill.

"About six-one."

"The lesbos the Hebrew has seen?"

"Too tall, if the kid's right."

Riordan ran a hand through his abundant hair. "The boy says he could not tell anything by the coat. What about the walk?"

"A mannish woman could screw that one up."

"No, no, I wasn't thinking about that. Everybody has a particular way of walking. It's like a kinetic signature, if you pay attention."

McKibbon knocked the ashes out of his pipe. "*If* the boy can remember, *if* he noticed enough to remember, what am I going to match the memory against?"

"That may come," said Riordan. "Anyway, ask him to focus on the walk. Tell me one other thing. No, two other things. The professor says he locked the front door before retiring, but he found it was unlocked when the uniformed boys came."

"So he says."

"So he says. Someone she knew. Either her spouse or someone else she knew."

"Hell, Lieutenant," McKibbon grinned, "I figured that one out right off—without any help at all."

Riordan smiled back. "Let me try you on this. The woman could not do without her coffee, all the more so when she was working. She had a deadline that night. There was a coffee cup, of course, on the kitchen table?"

McKibbon frowned. "Shit. The manuscript was there, and the typewriter, but no cup."

"Really?" Riordan reached for the gin. "Now what do you suppose ever happened to that cup?"

9 A cold, bright noon on Waverly Place. Behind the counter at the Ferdinand Morton Memorial Bookstore, Emma was writing down names. Writing them down and crossing them out. "Randolph," she said aloud. "They'd call him Randy. Got to be more solid than that. Bama wants his father's name. Lester. Soft. Besides, I'd be thinking of his father every time I see that boy. That cold, sour white face in his family album. No. God, no. Make it his middle name, if it has to be. Michael. I always did like Michael. Mike. Nobody messes with somebody named Mike."

A tall, thin, young black man in a black raincoat came in.

"Can I help you?" Emma said.

"Just looking." He showed his teeth.

She went back to the list, writing "Michael Dixon" large, writing it small, until the knife touched her hand.

"Do it quick, do it fast, and you'll last," the young man said softly. "All you got, wherever you got it."

"God damn!" Emma straightened up. "You black, and I'm black, and you're gonna take what I worked for. God damn! You listen to me. You get out of here right now, and that'll be the end of it. Or you're going to be in big trouble!"

"No shit." He smiled. "You got until right now, cunt, or the way you gonna look, that skinny white dude ain't gonna want you no more, no way. *Now!*"

Emma grabbed his hand, and in the astonishment of

her strength, he loosened his grip on the knife. With a terrifying cry of fear and rage, she snatched it and struck at his face.

"My eye!" he screamed. "You cut out my eye!" Moaning, with blood pouring through the fingers of the hand that he had pressed onto his right eye, the young man in the black raincoat ran out of the bookstore.

Emma, biting her lips, closed and locked the store and strode toward Washington Square. Near the fountain, she went up to a clump of young black men listening to a very large, very loud radio.

"I want Barney!" Emma shouted.

They ignored her.

Emma yanked the radio from the hands of one of the men, shut it off and said, in fury, "I want Barney!"

"Don't know no Barney," one of them said languidly. "You don't give me back that radio, bitch,"—his speech was still slow—"I'm gonna call the cops." His companions laughed. "Or maybe,"—he looked at Emma carefully, walking around her—"or maybe, you can keep it, you want it so bad, and then you got to give me something, right?" His companions laughed harder.

Emma raised the radio as high as she could, threw it to the ground as hard as she could and walked away. Two of the young men started after her, but the one who had been holding the radio said, "Leave it to Barney. He gotta know the bitch or she wouldn't be saying his name. Shee-it. That was a damn good radio. Well," he laughed, "it was last year's model. Might as well go shopping."

Emma had walked over to a bench where she sat, straight up, breathing hard, tapping her foot, her eyes glaring.

After a few minutes, she saw the huge man, the earring in his right ear, ambling toward her.

"Well, how do you do?" Barney said jovially as he sat

down. "A long time, girl. Such a long time. I see you in that store when I go down that street, time to time, but I figure I would not be welcome so, heavy in heart, I pass on by. I told you and I told you, that OD had nothing to do with me. Your cousin—yeah, Denton, that was his name—he got that shit somewhere else. You got to know that, girl. Way I cut, everybody safe."

Emma sat even straighter, and then got up. Standing in front of Barney, pointing a long finger at him, she said, speaking hard and quick, "One of your animals came in and pulled a knife on me. I cut him. I cut him real good. I do not want any of your animals in my place again. You hear me?"

Barney roared. "You cut him? Ain't that a bitch. Yeah, you always had balls. Speaking in the idiom, you know. My, my, my." He kept shaking his head in admiration. "You always were stronger than you look. Like a panther. Yeah. But Emma, mad as you are, and you got the right, Emma, how do you know it was one of my boys?"

"Don't fuck around with me,"—she looked down at Barney—"I've seen him with you. I knew I'd seen him somewhere, and it was with you. Right here. One of your famous junior executives."

"What makes you so sure it was the same boy, Emma?"

"He looks like a lizard, asshole. Now, you hear me? You keep them out of my place!"

Barney stretched. "Let me tell you something, Emma. You're dealing from nothing. You can't make me do a fucking thing. But, I like you. Always liked you. Full of sass. So, I am going to give the order. You got nothing more to worry about. Not from my boys, anyway. Nothing I can do about the free-lancers, you know."

Emma kept staring at him.

"And, just to show good faith,"—Barney poked Emma in the thigh and winced as she smacked his hand away—

"I am going to make that order ret-ro-ac-tive, so that boy is going to have to be punished for breaking my rules." Barney chuckled. "What you left of him. All rightee, anything else I can do for you?"

Her hands on her hips, Emma said slowly and distinctly, "Kiss my ass. Don't you wish you could, sucker." And she walked away.

"If I want to, I will," Barney muttered, and then giggled. "She cut him. Tyrone let a girl cut him. Boy needs a lesson. A good one. Damn, wish I could have seen that. That is some girl. My, my, my. She like you, Barney. Yeah, that's what she's saying. Kiss my ass, huh?" He watched her across the park. "If I want to, I will. If I want to."

In a glassed-in cubicle just off the newsroom, the round, black editor shook his head. "It's not going to run," he said smoothly. "There's nothing there."

"It's *all* there," Shannon Leahy snapped. "That's as much as the police know so far."

"Which is nothing,"—the editor fingered his red silk tie—"and you say nothing about how come they know nothing."

"It's a *news* story, Ray; it's not an op-ed piece."

"That's right, and you left out the key part of the news. Why don't they know anything by now? Anything at all? Here is a woman, murdered in her own kitchen, the wife of a professor, and," he smiled, "of a privileged color. So we should be seeing the Department at its very finest, moving right along on the track of the perpetrator. But what *do* we see? We see nothing. Or, as you put it so generously, 'The investigation is proceeding.' "

"What am I supposed to do," she asked sharply, "show them how to break the case?"

"You are not supposed to write something that reads

as if they wrote it. For openers, why didn't they book the husband? If this had happened uptown, under exactly the same set of circumstances, they would have busted the husband in a minute. So who's the professor's rabbi? Or didn't he even need one, given who he is and where he lives? Either way, that's news, and it's not in your story."

"Ray, it doesn't work like that." Shannon lit a cigarette. "Certainly not in a homicide case. If they took him in, he'd have clammed up. This way, they can keep working on him."

"Uh-huh," the editor said.

"Fuck you, Ray!" Shannon stood up. "Why the hell don't you assign this to a black reporter?"

"Shannon, I'm so glad you agree with me. I already have."

Green waited for him to start choking. Randazzo had put his whole hand into the apothecary jar, grabbed up all the sour balls it could hold and shoved them all into his mouth. But Randazzo's bel canto roar resumed without the slightest impediment.

"You let Stubblefield walk out of here." He pushed a finger close to Green's chest. "Okay, you had nothing to hold him on. BUT THEN YOU FORGOT ABOUT HIM. YOU NEVER TALKED TO HIM AGAIN!"

Green bit down on his cigar. "I did not forget about him. I tried to find him, but he'd disappeared."

"TOO LATE YOU TRIED TO FIND HIM." Randazzo stared at the photographs on his desk.

"You're the one who sets the priorities, Lieutenant," Green said icily. "You're the one who said the Ginsburg case came before everything else."

Randazzo bared his teeth in what might have been a smile. "And you're the one who said you don't play those games. Every corpse gets equal priority with you, the rummy in the ash can and the chief administrative judge —we should be so lucky."

"I try not to play those games," Green said, "but when your orders are so incessantly loud and clear, it's hard not to be influenced, you know."

Randazzo spread his hands and looked imploringly at the ceiling. "It's my fault. He loses this Stubblefield, and it's my fault."

"Weren't those your orders?" Green glared at the lieutenant. "Ginsburg *über alles.*"

"What does that have to do with the price of milk? Why are you a detective and not some *shlimazl* in uniform? Because you can think! That's what you get paid for. *Thinking.* So, if you were thinking, whatever the hell my orders were, you wouldn't have forgotten Stubblefield. Schmuck! Whether Stubblefield knew something or not, those primitives down there figured he did. Because we brought him in, right? And then we let him go. So if we let him go, they figure he must have told us something. So he got it last night. You seen these?" Randazzo pushed the photographs toward Green.

The detective, nodding, did not pick them up.

"Take another look!" Randazzo hit his desk with his knuckles, and hit it again. "Nice, efficient job. Straight in Stubblefield's throat. Poor bastard tried to pull the knife out, then he got the bullet in the back of the head—God forbid he shouldn't bleed to death fast enough. Go ahead, take another look."

"So what do you want me to do?" Green said, ignoring the photographs. "Leave the Ginsburg case with Sam and go back to the *bodega* killings? I'll lean on Domingo and get him to tell me why he fingered Stubblefield in the first place."

Randazzo ran his hand so hard through his hair that

Green expected a clump of it to come out. "Your fucking Domingo got this guy killed by getting him in here so somebody would think he told us something."

"Domingo thought it was good information," Green said. "If he was used, he didn't know it. But now he owes us. I'll find out whatever Domingo knows."

"The fuck you will!" Randazzo banged the desk with his fist. "First, you got nothing to do with the *bodega* killings anymore. Second, from now on, you—and everybody else here—are to have nothing whatever to do with Domingo. Except for busting him, which I would like a lot. A whole lot."

Both Green's hands were now fists. "You've never seen Domingo. You don't know anything about him. What you're telling me is that my judgment isn't worth shit. This guy broke some good cases for us, and now you're sitting there saying you *know* he set Stubblefield up. How do you know? What do you know just sitting there?"

Randazzo grinned. "You know why I know so much? Because I got brains in my ass. I got brains all over. That's *why* I'm sitting here. And I'll tell you something else I know. Your Domingo is a dead man. If not today, next week, next month. Aw, look at your face. What's the matter? You can't do anything without that snitch?"

"Listen,"—Green got up—"if you find my work unsatisfactory—"

"Siddown," Randazzo said amiably. "We all make mistakes. I made a couple myself, back in fifth-grade math. You don't think that's funny? All right. Even Riordan made some mistakes."

"No," said Green, "that couldn't be. Next you'll be telling me Garibaldi was busted for sodomy."

"Watch it. Yeah, Riordan blew a few. He wouldn't

admit it. He was just as stubborn as you. Anyway, if nobody tells you about your mistakes, you'll make them again. You don't have to kiss my hand. You want some sour balls?"

Green started to say no, but then put out his hand.

"One last thing," Randazzo said. "I am now getting regular calls from the Commissioner because he is getting regular calls from his sister who lives two streets away from Ginsburg, and she is kvetching. Oh boy, is she kvetching. Noah, I don't see no movement."

"I've seen cases in the files," Green said, "that took months. Some of them took a year or more. And until they broke, there didn't seem to be any movement at all.

"Now, these particular cases I'm talking about were all caught by one guy. He had a hell of a record. He never gave up, long as it took, and when he broke those cases, he broke them good. They were all convictions. Well, nearly all. You know, I bet there were a lot of times along the way when *his* commander was saying, 'Hey, what the hell's going on, there's no movement—' "

The lieutenant laughed. "You're talking about the one and only Fortunato Randazzo! You know what Riordan used to say when he got impatient with me because nothing seemed to be going on with my cases? He used to say, 'I figured it out, Fortunato. You're waiting until Resurrection Day so there'll be no mistakes, because then each victim can finger his own executioner.' Anyway, Noah, you're smarter than I thought—with your defensive research. Some day, when we got time, I'll fill you in on some of those cases. Stuff that doesn't get into the files.

"Yes, sir,"—the lieutenant made himself comfortable in his chair—"that must have been a real education, going through the Randazzo Files. Should have been a

TV series. But they did *Columbo,* so that's got to be the one wop series for the next fifty years.

"Okay," Randazzo beamed at Green, "so from now on, whenever you get stuck, just figure out what Fortunato Randazzo would have done." The lieutenant rose. "And that means you got no excuses no more."

10 Walking through Washington Square Park on the way to the jazz club on Bleecker Street, Green took in the usual clusters of hustlers, dealers, and predators of less immediately discernible intents. Sitting alone on a bench was a tall, thin, black teenager in a black raincoat. One eye was bandaged, and there was a fresh, ugly wound in the cheek under that eye. It looked almost as if a letter had been carved there, but Green couldn't be sure.

Looking at his watch, Green sat down on a bench at the far end of the park from where the teenager was. Then he got up, walked slowly around the bench and sat down once more. In a few minutes, a greasy-looking black man in his late thirties came toward him. Almost toothless, prancing rather than walking along, he stopped at the other end of Green's bench; and looking in the opposite direction from the detective, he took a seat.

"This is stupid," Green said. "They know who I am, so why do you insist on meeting me here?"

The black man laughed. "Oh, you know why. You've been around so long, you got to know why. I want them to know I got some clout, I got powerful friends. And then, soon as I leave you, I tell them how I jerked you off. So I got double clout. They see I go right up to the man and jive him about. They see I got smarts the man don't know nothing about. So what you want?"

"What you got? It's your dime."

"Oh yeah. Gonna be a war. Some of the cats here been selling shit that ain't shit, you know, all kinds of shit that ain't shit. Well, some of the cats that bought that shit that ain't shit, they come by this afternoon to get a refund, you know, and they got the shit beat out of them, real shit. They gonna come back, and somebody gonna be killed, certain. So I figured that's your department."

"They say they were going to come back?"

"Oh yeah, they say that, while they picking up their teeth. But they don't say when."

Green looked around the park. "Okay, I'll make a call."

"I better be clean next couple of days, huh?" the black man snickered. "But you know, I hate to see anybody stomped on. Even them guineas. You know, sun shines on every motherfucker and it rains on every mother-fucker, and everybody's ass points to the goddamned ground, so we all alike, and we all ought to live till we die. Natural, you know."

"I know," Green said, lighting a cigar. "There's a saying in the Talmud—you know what the Talmud is?"

"Yeah, I was a *Shabbes goy* for a while when I was a kid in Brooklyn."

"Okay, it says in the Talmud that he who saves a single life, it is as if he saved an entire world. On the other hand, what are you saving down *here?* It's like saving skinfuls of deadly germs. Wouldn't the world be a whole lot better off if you didn't save them and let them stomp each other into the ground?"

"I ain't God, Captain. You ain't neither. Anyway, you putting me on."

"Yeah, you got it. Tell me, the kid on the bench back there with the bandaged eye."

"Tyrone. Don't know his other name."

"Isn't he one of Barney's boys?"

"Was. He among the unemployed now."

"Why?"

"They don't talk outside themselves, you know. But sometime they talk a little loud inside themselves. Tyrone did something to a friend of Barney. Tyrone did not know it was a friend, which was too bad for Tyrone."

"Barney had him worked over?" Green asked.

"That Arthur. You know that Arthur?"

"The West Indian, the jogger?"

"Brrrrr,"—the black man made a show of shivering—"I don't want to talk about him no more. The boy, he got kicked out after Arthur got through with him. That's what hurts him. Hurts him real bad. More than what Arthur did. How's he going to move up in the world now?"

"Is that a letter on his cheek?"

"I ain't gone that close to look," the black man said. "That's a mean boy, Tyrone. And he's lots meaner now."

"Okay." Green dropped two folded twenty-dollar bills on the ground. The black man bent over to tie his shoe and palmed them.

"I'd of gotten more," the black man said, "if they'd gone and killed somebody and I'd told you who did it."

Green smiled. "You mean it's not enough reward to have saved an entire world?" He dropped another folded twenty-dollar bill and walked off.

Ten minutes later, Green was leaning against the wall next to the narrow door of the Blue Light, which was actually a large cave of a room downstairs. "Long time, Noah." A tall, broad-shouldered, gray-haired black man with a white goatee poked him in the shoulder. "You official tonight, or just having fun?"

"It's my night off," the detective said.

"That don't mean nothing. Not with you old-timers. Catch the tenor with Art Blakey. New blood. Nineteen goddamn years old! Sure wish Mingus was still around. He would love this cat. I mean he's bad. And he's got the chops to be bad with. I'll bring him over later. Always helps to know the heat."

Shannon Leahy got out of a cab, smiling. On top of her red hair was a pair of glasses. She saw Green's eyes there. "Oh my God,"—she felt for the glasses and put them in a case in her purse—"I just finished a rewrite."

"I liked the look of that," Green said. "Purposeful."

"Oh yuh, I got my eye on the ball, all right, except it keeps curving. But who wants fat pitches all the time? Me, that's who."

Downstairs, they sat at a table against the wall. When the band came on, Green identified the players and told her something of their histories as they tuned up and waited for a straggler. The reporter ordered a brandy, the detective a double scotch and water. "I don't want to flag a waiter while they're playing," he said.

Shannon Leahy looked at him with a slight smile. "My husband was very considerate of performers too. He'd order three doubles at a time, he was such a good audience."

Under the table, Green punched his thigh. "I'm really on a streak. I keep missing things. I just didn't figure you for being married."

"You figured right." She lit a cigarette. "That was a long time ago."

"So was mine," Green said. "It's hard to believe it ever was. It's like some other guy did it."

"Yeah," she said. "Except I have a permanent reminder." She smiled. "My boy, Joey. He's ten. The marriage was terrible, but look what I got to keep. You have any kids?"

Green shook his head. "She didn't want to interrupt her career."

"Which was?"

"Slipping and sliding."

"Huh?" The reporter leaned forward.

"You don't listen to country music." Green finished his drink. "Ruth was a comparison shopper. She was always on the lookout for someone who is, as they say, great in bed. Greater. Greatest. Someone who makes the earth move, you know. I should have dropped out very early, I was never a contender, but I had that thing that holds so many disgusting marriages together."

"You still wanted her?"

"Hell, no. I mean inertia. Finally she kicked me out. She found the right Cracker Jack box. But he was a shopper too, and didn't stay long. Ain't that a shame?"

Green, waiting, looked at her.

"My marriage drowned, Noah. Corny as that. He was one hell of a reporter, so long as he could keep his head off the typewriter. He was sick, that's all, and I didn't want to be that kind of nurse anymore."

"He still in town?"

"Not that we know. And I'm sure not looking."

The music started, and halfway through the first number, the nineteen-year-old tenor, black, short, muscular, holding his horn at an angle away from his body, came up to the mike and, from the first huge, whooping cry, stunned the room into silence. His sound was hard, penetrating, hungry. At times, he phrased like an old-time, shouting preacher; but then, zooming outside the chords, his growls, screeches and demonic whispers were like, Green thought, those of a dybbuk. Maybe Nat Turner was inside him, or Charlie Parker, or Barney. But Barney was not yet dead.

"God," Shannon Leahy said when the song was over. "To have all that inside you, and I bet he was just warming up. Gee, you see somebody like that walking down the street and you have no idea—"

"It's a good thing he plays a horn," Green said. "What would he do with all that ferociousness otherwise?"

"You've got tunnel vision," she said. "It must be an occupational disease. He could be a teacher or a preacher or a cop or a detective. Yeah, he could be a detective."

"You think I've got what he's got in me?"

"Yeah," she smiled. "A different beat maybe, slower, but just as ferocious. Somewhere in there."

At the end of the set, Green ordered two more double scotches and another brandy. The gray-haired man with the white goatee brought the young tenor player to the table.

"Charlie Hansen, the manager of this joint," Green introduced the older man to the reporter.

"And this is Drew," Hansen said, "Drew Hall."

"That is the most powerful jazz I've heard in a long time," Green told the tenor player.

"That is your word," Hall, smiling, said softly. "But thank you."

"I should have said black music," Green said, bridling at Shannon Leahy's amused look.

"All words set limits, Mr. Green," the tenor player said. "Perhaps it's not necessary to put labels on what we hear."

"That's what Trane said." Green looked at Shannon Leahy.

"Yes, John Coltrane did say that," Hall nodded. "Often. That's one reason he went so far. None of us caught up to him yet."

"*You* will," the reporter said.

"No," Hall said flatly. "Not if I try to. You know what I mean?"

Shannon Leahy said, "My father used to say, 'If you don't want to join the throng, you got to write your own song.'"

Drew Hall grinned. "You are very advanced. It's been a pleasure meeting you." He turned to Green. "And you too, sir."

"I didn't know you were so hip," Green said after Hall and the club's manager had left. "I felt like your uncle from Des Moines."

Leahy looked at her watch. "Well, uncle, it's time for me to get home."

"I'll see you home," said Green as he waved to a waiter.

"I don't want to take you out of your way. I'll get a cab."

"Sorry," Green said.

"Oh Jesus." Leahy shook her head. "Of course you can see me home." She laughed. "I wasn't sure you wanted to, and you weren't sure I wanted you to. Isn't that silly? At our age."

"*Our* age? You must be thirty."

"Direct hit."

"So I could be your father."

Shannon looked at Noah somewhat quizzically. "You're a very self-conscious man, Noah. But somehow, it adds to your charm."

"What charm?" He affected a growl.

Partly suppressing a smile, she looked into Green's eyes, making him quite uncomfortable. "Remember what the man said, Noah. All words set limits. Let's go. It's not only that the babysitter has to get home by eleven-thirty, but Joey, if he can keep himself up, starts getting very worried if I'm not home by then. He figures I'm crumpled up somewhere with a knife in me."

Green saw Kathleen Ginsburg in the kitchen, and got up from the table. "I hope you're careful about whom you go out with."

Shannon laughed. "You're funny. You're a very funny man."

11 Three o'clock the next morning, Bama, coming from a song-swapping session in a Soho loft, was flowing home. And some might have said floating, if they had drunk as well and as deeply as he all night long, and now heard him in the street.

Oh, Satan, he came by my hear-rrr-t,
Throw brickbats in the door.
Bama stopped, ducked and watched in joy.
But Master JE-SUS! come with the brush,
Make cleaner than before.

From a doorway, two of Barney's myrmidons, scavenging on their own time, considered the streets' last offering before dawn.

"Whatever he on, he gone. We can take him with one thumb."

"How come he singing like he's black?"

"Everybody do that nowadays."

"I dunno. Maybe he be a albino. Bad luck."

"Say who?"

"Say my mama. I got a feeling, that's all. Maybe he be crazy. You never know what crazy people do."

"Shee-it, he don't look like he got two dollars anyway. Motherfucker don't know how lucky he is."

Shivering in the wind from the river, the two night creatures hurried toward a diner on the corner.

"Pimps stay warm, you know."

"We got to leave Barney, we want to do that."

"Yeah." He felt his throat. "Well, somebody gonna get Barney one day, and then we be free."

His companion laughed. "Again?"

In the middle of the street behind them, Bama was directing a huge choir:
Brothers, don't you hear the horn?
He leaned toward the bank of singers on his right.
Yes, Lord, I hear the horn.
Swaying now to the left, Bama, palms up, sang
Sisters, don't you hear the horn?
Yes, Lord, I hear the horn.
Barney's boys looked back. "Don't hear nothin," one of them shouted. "Got my head inside your mama!" Giggling, they went on.

Bama gave no sign of having heard anything but the voices immediately around him. Lifting his arms as high as they could go,
Mourners don't you hear the horn?
Then, bending close to the ground, singing soft and high,
Yes, Lord, I hear the horn.
It sound like my Daddy's horn.
Dismissing the choir with applause, Bama, after a sparkling if erratic jig, a reel and a long, gliding waltz, moved on toward home.

Opening the door with great care, hearing nothing, not even Merle Haggard, seeing the living room empty, tiptoeing to the bedroom, empty too, and beginning to tremble, yelling "Emma! Emma! Em-ma!," stumbling, his throat closing, to the kitchen and there, lying on the floor, curved, her head on her right arm, Emma. In her back, plunged in deep, a knife. And wounds on her neck, and her arms, and Lord God, everywhere else, and leaning over her, he saw, across the room, Merle Haggard, his throat slit, looking at him with a terrible shame.

Bama kneeled by his wife and found no breath, no pulse. Emma's eyes were wider than he had ever seen them. The refrigerator door was open, a bottle of milk had smashed on the floor. He looked into her eyes again and there was a sound, a harsh tearing at his throat, breaking free into a wail, a howling, as he closed his eyes and banged his head against the floor, and then there was silence.

His face closed, Bama got up, started walking to the door, stopped, went to the phone and dialed Noah Green's home number.

"Emma's gone," he said tonelessly. "I just found her. I just found her. I just found a knife in her."

Green sounded as if he were strangling. "Be right there."

"She's so still. How can Emma be so still?"

"Bama, stay there. Stay right there."

The fiddler hung up the phone, bent over Emma again, looked at Merle Haggard, poured a water glass full of bourbon, poured it into the sink and left the house.

Sam McKibbon, who'd gone to sleep early, was up at two that morning, wandering. He'd stopped in at an after-hours joint in East Harlem, which had led to a poker game, which had taken most of his bread, and now he was in the all-night diner near his Chelsea apartment. McKibbon ordered another cup of coffee, lit his pipe, felt the crack and took the pipe out of his mouth.

Shit. Another stem done gone. Coffee cup. Crime-scene guys did not take any coffee cup. Did not see any coffee cup, except for the ones in the dishwasher, and they'd been washed.

He took another pipe out of his pocket and slowly filled it. *What was it Mr. Goldfarb used to say when we fucked up in math? "If you don't know where you're going, any road will take you there." Okay, Sam, take a road.*

Connie's. Dead end. Noah struck out with the two lesbos. Wait a minute. The fag. Whipple. He hangs out there sometimes. Violence is not Whipple's shtick, Noah says. Shit, something snaps, violence is anybody's shtick. Ain't nobody don't want to do somebody in one time or another.

At least the fag may know something. Snitches don't tell everything they know. Didn't think of Whipple. Snitches become part of the woodwork. Hell of a good reason to become a snitch.

McKibbon shrugged, got up, looked at his watch, put on his coat and headed downtown. *I'll get that Horowitz kid on his way to school. Then I'll check in.*

"I've been trying," the thin boy with the cloud of red hair said across the table in the coffee shop on the corner of the street where Kathleen Ginsburg had also resided. "All I can see is the back of somebody short."

"Any particular way the person walked?" McKibbon asked.

The boy frowned. "Kind of hunched over, I think. But it was cold that night."

"Anything else? About the walk?"

The boy shook his head. "If I could see it again. Maybe. I mean, if there was someone you thought might be that person, and I could watch that someone walk. Maybe something would come back then."

"Do you think Mrs. Ginsburg and this other person saw you?" McKibbon was looking at the boy's bright red hair.

"I wasn't hiding or anything. I was about to go up the steps, and there's that street lamp right there, you know."

"Were you wearing a cap or a hat or anything?"

"I always go bare-headed. Anything on my head gives me a headache."

"I'll be in touch, Adam," McKibbon said. "We're going to try an experiment."

"What kind?"

"We're going to see if we can bring back your memory. Or somebody's memory. But you're game, right?"

"Sure," the boy said. "Anything you want. I mean, you can't let the killer get away with it. So, any amount of time it takes is fine with me."

"Hold on," the detective said. "I'm not going to be responsible for you blowing your SATs. This can all be done after school. And it won't take long. Just be sure you don't change on me and take to wearing something on that fine head of hair."

Bama had left no trail. Nothing. The band he usually worked with was rehearsing that afternoon at the Lone Star Café, a hangout at the northern end of the Village for transplanted Texans and folks who liked to think of themselves as Texans. A large, stagy room with a balcony and a grand staircase, it had terrible acoustics and did good business.

"You got a competitor on Emma's case," the steel-guitar player said to Green when the band took a break. A bulging man with thinning blond hair and a broad, unfriendly smile, he had long irritated the detective who had never been able to understand Bama's close friendship with him.

"I know that," Green said, lighting a cigar.

"How's old Haggard?" the steel-guitar player asked.

"He'll live. It looked awful, but the vet stitched it up okay. All the spirit's out of him though."

"Where is he?"

"With me. I'm minding him for Bama. You tell Bama that, Carl."

The steel-guitar player rubbed his nose with his free hand. "Bama ain't dumb, you know that. None of us gonna see him until he's done what he has to do."

"If he knows what he's doing," Green said. "And even if he does, Bama's got no license to kill."

"Oh, I dunno," Carl said slowly, "even a jury in New York City might think different."

"If you do hear from him,"—Green locked eyes with Carl—"tell him I know a lot more than he does, so he ought to get in touch. Unless he really doesn't give a fuck about who killed Emma, and is just doing a king-of-the-jungle number. You tell him I said that. In exactly those words."

Carl smiled. "I don't remember good. You tell him. And you know something, you don't know shit more than he does. 'Cause if you did, you'd have somebody in a cell right now, whether you had anything solid on him or not, just to keep him from being torn into stinking little pieces by Bama."

Green poked Carl in the chest. "I want that message delivered. Without comment. Or I'll be dogging your ass, forever." He was about to poke him again, but Carl slapped the finger away.

"Last time a Jew boy poked a finger at me," Carl growled, "I bit it off, and I planted it and a money tree come up. I've just about run out of that money."

Green dropped his cigar, still lit, into the guitar. "Next time, I'll plant *you*. Right alongside your Lord. Give Bama the message."

A fist in his pocket, Green went out the door of the

Lone Star and was walking swiftly uptown when a thin, high, rather melodious voice called softly, "Hey, not so fast, man. It's going to attract attention if I'm chasing you."

A short, chunky man, with yellow-looking eyes in a soft brown face, caught up to Green.

"I figured you'd want the news," Domingo smiled, "even though the lieutenant put me on the shit list."

"Listen, Domingo,"—Green glared at him—"I want to talk to you about Stubblefield."

"Later, man. Don't you want to hear what I got? Besides, the lieutenant's talking crazy about me and Stubblefield. You know me, Noah. I don't give you nothing phony that I *know* is phony. I thought I was giving you the straight stuff about Stubblefield. And maybe I was. Him getting killed don't necessarily mean he wasn't the one that took off the old man and the old lady in the *bodega.*"

"*Who* gave you Stubblefield's name?" Green's voice was no warmer.

"Man,"—Domingo looked quickly across the street—"minute I tell you, I am dead. You can do what you want, but I don't tell you that. You know when I'm serious. You can pull me in, you can lock me up for a hundred years, but I ain't committing suicide, you know. Now, you want my news, Noah, or not? You never screwed me, man, so I'm doing something for you. I know the lady in the bookstore was a friend of yours."

"We're still going to have a long talk, just you and me, about Stubblefield. But go ahead."

"That boy, Tyrone, that boy with the fucked-up eye you was asking about down at the park."

Green shook his head. "Jesus, I could just as well go down there with a public-address system."

"You did," Domingo giggled. "When you talk to that

dancing spade with no teeth in his head hanging around down there, you're talking to the whole fucking world. Anyway, reason Tyrone got that eye and got thrown out of Barney's army is he tried to mess with that lady in the bookstore. The lady got all hot and told Barney what Tyrone did. Barney liked that lady, so that's why Tyrone is on the outside. And that's why Tyrone got that letter on his face too."

"What's the letter?"

"C. For cunt. That was Tyrone's favorite word."

Green lit a cigar. "So Tyrone killed Emma because she brought Barney down on him?"

"Don't ask me, man. I just give the news. And that news been traveling. May even have gotten to that fiddle player. All kinds of musicians down there, in the park." Domingo smiled. "But you didn't know why Tyrone got messed up, right? Till I just told you."

Green nodded in agreement as Domingo beamed with satisfaction.

"Okay," Domingo said, "you don't tell the lieutenant I seen you, and I won't tell the lieutenant I seen you." He giggled. "Just wanted to show you I was still your man. Have a nice day."

Domingo walked off. Green started after him but stopped, felt for his gun and continued uptown.

12 Green raced up the stairs and into the squad room. Furious at himself for being out of breath, he leaned on a desk, saw McKibbon and wheezed, "We got to find Barney. Right now."

McKibbon held up his hand, and then pointed his forefinger at Randazzo's office. The door was closed. "Barney found us. Said he would talk only to the head man, and that's what he's doing right now. Would you let me know what the hell's going on before Randazzo does?"

Green quickly told him Domingo's news. "That fucking Tyrone killed her, and we got to get him before Bama. And Barney's our bloodhound."

"One thing," McKibbon said. "Why didn't Emma tell you about what happened in the store?"

"Because I used to nag her about being alone there. And the nagging would have gotten worse. Besides, she figured she didn't need any help with a punk like that."

They crossed the room to Randazzo's office. Green knocked as he opened the door. Randazzo was looking at Barney with loathing as the huge black man popped a handful of sour balls into his mouth.

"We put it on the radio," Randazzo said gloomily to Green. "Squad car should be there any minute. You know what I'm talking about?"

"I just found out," said Green. Barney waved languidly at him, but when he caught McKibbon's cold eye, he dropped his hand.

"I don't know if Tyrone still lives there," Barney spoke to Green. "Soon as I heard about Emma, I went by there, but no sign of the boy. And some of my people been checking ever since. Nothin. Nobody around there has seen him since—since it happened. Funny thing for me to be saying, but I wish you guys had him."

"You'd have brought him in if you'd found him?" McKibbon glanced at the clock on Randazzo's desk.

"Yeah," Barney said. "I really worked with that boy. He was like a sewer rat when I found him. Vicious little mother. I thought I was finally making something out of him. But he reverted to type. Shit. You got to believe,"—Barney turned so that he faced Green directly—"that it tears me up, what happened to Emma. Well, fuck it, I don't care what you believe. But I am sick, man. Still, I don't want Tyrone, piece of shit that he is, to get it this way, even after what he done."

"You're pretty fucking solicitous after what *you* had done to him," Green said.

"Don't know what you're talking about." Barney eyed the sour-ball jar, which Randazzo pulled out of his reach. "But Jesus, God knows what that fiddler's gonna do. Could tear Tyrone's balls off, for openers. I mean a cat like that, wow, he's really *dangerous.*"

"Gotta be more to it than that." McKibbon blew some pipe smoke in Barney's direction. "You didn't come in just because you wanted to save that little prick's balls."

"Mr. Richmond," Randazzo said sourly, "is here to show his respect for the Department. He came to help us find the boy, but also for another reason. Tell them, you scumbag."

Barney stiffened for a moment, then smiled. "I pay

dues when I have to. Trot out your other words too, Commander, so long as it makes you feel better."

"Asshole," Randazzo said.

"Tell it!" Barney spread his arms like a preacher. "Let me hear you signify!"

"You eat shit!" Randazzo said.

"Aw,"—Barney leaned back against the wall—"you're not in your prime this morning, Commander." He looked at McKibbon. "Lend him some words, brother, some of our words. Make him feel better."

"You know what I'd like better than anything in this whole world?" McKibbon leaned toward Barney.

"No, what's that, brother?"

"I'd like to watch you die. For a long time. A month maybe. Maybe longer."

Barney laughed.

"What's the other reason he's here for?" Green asked Randazzo, but Barney answered. "I could be on that crazy man's list too. You go after one of Fagin's boys that cold and hard, you got to get Fagin too if you want to finish the job. I mean, he's gonna figure I'm the cause of that boy, you dig? Hadn't been for me, that boy might never have come near Emma. Could have stayed up-town or in Bed-Stuy, or who knows where? Man as wild as Bama, you don't know what he's gonna think. But you see, he associates me with that boy, so it figures he's gonna blame me for that boy. Now, it ain't that I'm asking for police protection—"

"Wait a second!" Randazzo roared. "It would be such a pleasure to give you police protection, I would assign myself to the first shift. I would take a double shift."

"And when I sleep," Barney chuckled, "you put something real good in my pocket. Naw, it ain't like I'm asking for police protection. I'm gonna protect myself by being real scarce for a while. Can't take chances with a crazy man. But, I just want you folks to know that if he finds me, I will have to defend myself. I want that on the record. If the dude comes after me, I'm gonna have to take care of myself. You got it?"

"You come here for a license?" Green yelled.

"Shoosh," Randazzo said. "I have already told Mr. Richmond that nothing he has said is worth putting on any record except insofar as, in a court of law, it will establish his intent to kill."

There was a knock on the door, and a detective called in. "They entered the apartment. Nobody there. Some clothes, but that's all."

No one spoke for a while. "He's probably long gone on some bus," Green said.

"Hee, hee, hee," Barney said, examining his fingernails. "I just hope that crazy man leaves enough of Tyrone so the boy can be identified."

The next afternoon, Sam McKibbon and the redheaded boy were coming out of the subway in Soho.

"That candy store." McKibbon pointed diagonally across the street. "He picks up the *Post* there every afternoon around four. We just got a little time. I'm going to be in that bookstore behind us."

"And what am I going to be doing?" Adam Horowitz asked.

"You're going to be in the candy store buying comic books." McKibbon shook his head. "My abject apologies. Buy what you want." He handed the boy a five-dollar bill. "Now, take a quick look at him and then watch him carefully once he leaves and walks down the street. Okay?"

Horowitz nodded; McKibbon walked into the bookstore and began to browse among the shelves near the window.

Looking at the magazine racks, Horowitz was annoyed. "You don't have *Scientific American?*" he asked the elderly woman behind the counter.

She did not. Nor did she have the *Bulletin of the Atomic Scientists, The Progressive* or *Inquiry.* The boy sighed and was about to pick up, with distaste, a copy of *Rolling Stone* when a soft, cheerful voice behind him said, "And how are you this afternoon, Mrs. Arricola?"

"Like always, Mr. Whipple, like always. I don't complain. All I ask is to get through the day."

"Me too," Whipple said, paying for the *Post.* "I can hardly wait till the sun goes down." As he was about to leave the store, Whipple noticed the boy, turned back and asked for a pack of Marlboros. As he went into his jacket pocket for the money, he looked in the general direction of the boy but did not seem to be focusing on anything in particular.

Soon after Whipple left the store, Horowitz went out and watched him walk down the block. When Whipple turned a corner, the boy crossed the street and was surprised to find McKibbon standing outside the bookstore.

"Wait," said McKibbon as the boy was about to speak. "Let's see if you got a base hit."

Coming back around the corner that he had just turned, Whipple stood, saw the boy and McKibbon and went straight down the street away from them.

"I'm afraid our friend is not going to sleep well tonight," McKibbon said.

"You think he recognized me?" Horowitz asked.

"I think he recognized *both* of us," McKibbon said. "That way he's not going to bother you."

"That's why you were waiting for me outside?"

"Uh-huh. If he had seen only you and figured you weren't in that store just to buy magazines, he might have gotten some rash ideas."

"But now he *knows* I wasn't there just to buy magazines," Adam said anxiously.

"Yup. And he also knows that *I* know you weren't there just to buy magazines. So if he wants to mess with you, he's gonna have to mess with me, and he doesn't want to do that. At all. So you've got nothing to worry about."

"I hate to tell you this," the boy said, "but I watched him walk down the street real carefully, and I can't say that's the person I saw with Mrs. Ginsburg the night she was killed. I can't say it for sure. I mean, he was hunched over just now, even though it's not that cold out today, but some people walk that way all the time."

"That's okay, kid," McKibbon said. "You've helped a lot. Now we just let him stew awhile. And then he and I will have a talk."

"He did it, huh?"

"One thing at a time. To recapitulate—something we detectives like to do—he got very interested in you just now because—and so far this is just an assumption—he remembered your grand head of red hair. So that *may* put him on the street with Mrs. Ginsburg the night of the murder. We still do not have him inside her kitchen later that night. But, one link at a time."

Moving out of Soho, north toward Greenwich Village, they were walking past an abandoned school and McKibbon suddenly stopped. In a far corner of the playground, a shoe was barely protruding from underneath a loose pile of debris—a broken bench, a tipped-over trash basket and rotting, empty cartons.

"Stay here," McKibbon said to the boy.

The detective walked over to the pile, peered into it and saw at the bottom, crumpled against the wall, a young black man, maybe nineteen, in a black raincoat. His head was down, the back of it shattered.

"Two bullets, maybe three." McKibbon closed his eyes for a moment, went back to the street and told Horowitz, "Okay, kid, better get home. I got some work here."

"Hey, I want to see." The boy moved toward the playground.

McKibbon grabbed him by the collar. "No, you don't. Believe me, you don't want to see what's in there. Or don't believe me, but get the hell out of here."

Horowitz, pouting, walked off. McKibbon went back into the playground, stared again at the dead black boy and said to him, "You sure did get even, Tyrone. Now, doesn't that make you feel better?"

That evening, mild for December, in the doorway of a men's store near the corner of Sixth Avenue and Eighth Street, a youthful string quartet was playing Mozart's Quartet no. 19 in C, the so-called *Dissonant* Quartet. Except that amid that corner's, that neighborhood's and that city's normal nighttime sounds, the clashing of these strings was so astonishingly gentling that all manner of predators, let alone citizens merely on the way to get fruit or coffee, were simply standing there—some smiling, some confounded by the eeriness of ordered, melodious passion.

Green, however, was not in the mood. Looking ceaselessly for a solo violinist in quite another idiom, he was about to walk by when he was tapped on the shoulder. Wheeling around, his hands clenched, Green saw a small, fragile man with a tight, angry face.

"What the hell's going on, Noah?" Crocker Whipple's voice was horse and agitated.

"Don't be uncool, my man." Green glanced toward an empty doorway up the street, proceeded there, and was soon joined by Whipple.

"I was tailed this afternoon." Whipple was indignant.

"Your partner put some Yid kid—sorry, I'm upset—on me. Why?"

"News to me," Green said. "You done something I don't know about?"

The small man bit his lip. "If you're going to lie to me, Noah, that's the end of it. What I do for you is dangerous enough as it is. But if you're going to play games with me, fuck it."

"It's a free country," Green said, looking through the passing crowd. "I accept your resignation."

"Why are you screwing me?" Whipple's fingers seemed to have no place to rest.

"We appreciate your long and generally reliable service, but we recognize that since your service was voluntary—"

"Voluntary, shit. We made a deal when you got me off that possession of obscene materials rap, and you sure been charging a hell of a lot of interest."

"Lovely pictures," Green kept watching the passersby. "Real lyrical stuff. Sweet, nimble boys fucking each other in the ass. And in color. You could see their little eyes gleam. But my favorite was that beautifully textured shot of the deep-black boy eating that big white cock. Was that your cock, Crocker?"

"Noah, will you please tell me what's going on? Look, forget what I just said. I'll stay on, but—"

"I'm sorry," Green said. "I already accepted your resignation. Regulations say that once a statement has been given, you can't reverse the paper flow."

"What paper flow, for Christ's sake? Noah, why are you doing this? I just got upset. I haven't been well lately anyway, and then to see McKibbon and this kid—"

"Got your period?" Green laughed. "Very unhip, what I just said, right? Vulgar. Just what you'd expect from a *big* Yid."

"Okay, you're entitled. For God's sake, what am I supposed to have done?"

"Beats me," Green said. He looked up at the Jefferson Market clock. "Yeah, amazing color. Never saw anything like those pictures you took. You gave a set to all those kids, I hope? I mean, it'll be so nice for them to be able to show those pictures to their misshapen grandchildren."

"Noah, I'll call you."

"Fuck off, fag. If I have a chance, I'll sit *shivah* for you."

"The fiddler's never seen me." Crocker Whipple, hunched up in a thick, green sweater, was watching a pacing Siberian tiger the next afternoon at the Bronx Zoo. "I can track Bama if he's still in the city."

"Oh, he's here," Barney said. "So long as I'm here, he's here." Barney turned away from the tiger and looked slowly around at the scattered clumps of people taking a winter trip to see some authentic animals. "Shit, if I can't make a cop by now, I ought to be in some other line of work. Nobody's paying any mind to us. They all civilians over there."

"You sure you never been tailed without knowing it?" Whipple asked.

Barney grinned. "Naw. I can smell a cop a mile away. They smell afraid, just like you smell afraid."

"They can do you without even showing up, you know." Whipple ignored the reference to himself. "How do you know they didn't bug the tiger? They got equipment can pick up a whisper in another state."

"They didn't know we were going to come over and see the tiger, smart-ass. They would have had to bug every animal in the joint. But you funnin' me. I just wanted to show you I can think right past you anyway."

"Okay." Whipple lit a cigarette. "I'll find Bama, provided you don't tell me what happens to him after I find him."

Barney smiled. "I bet you only a couple of people know what happened to Jimmy Hoffa, although more than just a couple of people were in on it, one way or another. Don't worry about it, little fart. I wouldn't tell you anyway. What I got in mind for that peckerwood, I might want to use again. So it's gotta stay secret."

"You got it all worked out?"

"Can't help poking and poking and poking, can you? Like a little white mouse. Yeah, I got it all worked out. Schmuck, you know the real reason I'm not gonna tell you?"

"Because then I'd have to end up the same way as him. That's why I said I didn't want to know."

"All rightee." Barney stretched. "We all set. You got the down payment. When you deliver, it's gonna be the biggest score you ever made." He looked down at Whipple, who seemed somewhere else. "Something eating on you? The Yid kid?"

Whipple nodded.

"That ain't nothing. I will send some of my associates to reason with him, hee, hee, and then you got nothing to worry about."

"Jesus, Barney, don't do that. That's all I need. It's like telling McKibbon to come and get me, and he will, whether he's got anything on me that'll stick or not. Anyone leans on the kid, that cop will be sure I had something to do with Kathleen Ginsburg."

Barney toyed with his earring. "I never figured you for murder. At least not that way. I can see you nibbling somebody to death, but wham, bam, thank you, ma'am, with a big knife, why, that ain't you, little fart."

"It's not what you think, Barney. Shit, that kid is the only connection between me and her."

"If it ain't what I think, what the hell difference does the kid make?"

"He's the first link."

"The first?" Barney grinned.

"Barney, this is my hassle. For God's sake, stay away from that kid. I don't want to stir them up. If I can wait them out—I mean, the kid is all they have."

"So you think." Barney dug a huge hand into a box of Cracker Jacks. "You don't look good, man. You better be sure you can handle this gig I just give you."

"I know how to take care of business. You know that, Barney. You better give me a number where I can always get to you fast."

The Siberian tiger had stopped pacing and was staring at Barney with considerable ill will. "Eat your heart out," he said to it cheerily, and turned to Whipple. "For a while, nobody's going to be able to get direct to me, fast or slow. I'm going into hibernation, hee, hee. But you call me where you always do, and somebody will get to *you* fast."

"Arthur?"

"Don't push, little fart." Barney started to walk away, then turned around. "Newspapers say the knife went all the way *in*. You must have been holding it in your mouth."

Crocker, hands jammed into his pockets, walked off quickly in the other direction.

Barney slapped his hands together, waved at the still-staring tiger and loped away.

13

Early Sunday morning on the lively upper West Side of Manhattan. A woman, screaming, "You fucking bastard! You rotten son of a bitch! Everything! I did everything! I did everything you wanted! I always did everything you wanted. What the hell *more* do you want?"

Green heard mumbling, but couldn't make out what the man was saying. He went to the window. Nothing. They must be in a doorway. Then the man, big and blond, in his late thirties, wearing only a light, dirty safari jacket in the cold, moved quickly onto the sidewalk, almost trotting away.

"Don't you come back!" the woman yelled. "Don't you ever come back, you cunt! Oh God!" she was sobbing.

Green scratched his head. He'd never heard that one before. He looked at the clock. Nine. He'd wanted to sleep Sunday away if he could. Shit. Couldn't go over and talk to Emma and the fiddler anymore. Too early for a movie. Anyway, there was nothing he wanted to see. Next Sunday, he'd be working, thank God.

He looked at the quart of J&B on the night table, and he remembered a collar years ago. A black trumpet player. The door hadn't even been locked. Green and his partner had just eased into the room, the musician had opened his eyes, seen them, closed his eyes, opened them again and said, "Just a second." He looked at them again and said, "Hey, would you get it? Under the bed. So you won't think I'm going for a piece."

Green had bent down, looked under the bed and seen a jug. "Can't get up without it," the musician said. Green handed him the jug, watched him take a long swallow, set it down carefully on the floor and slowly get up.

"You always start your day that way?" Green's partner had asked.

The musician frowned. "Gonna be awful bad—without this." He reached for the jug, took a longer swallow, and they put the cuffs on.

"One thing," the musician said. "It wasn't rape. I knowed her a long time."

"Tell your lawyer," Green had said.

Green stared at the scotch, went into the kitchen where Merle Haggard, his face to the wall, pretended to be asleep, and made some coffee. Taking a yellow legal pad and a felt-tip pen from off the refrigerator, he sat down and drew a vertical line, starting halfway across the top page. On the left side, he wrote 1) KATHLEEN; on the right, 2) EMMA. Green looked at the page. Then, under KATHLEEN, he wrote CROCKER, GINSBURG, THE LESBOS, CONNIE, and stopped. For a long time. He looked at a pack of cigars with distaste, opened it, and wrote ROBBER.

"Maybe if I did it in Yiddish," Green said aloud, "I'd find out something. If I knew Yiddish."

Under EMMA, he listed TYRONE, ROBBER and, with a mirthless grin, MERLE HAGGARD. "Fucking dog is so smart, he could have handled the knife with his teeth." Still looking at the sheet, rapping his knuckles on the table, lighting a cigar, spitting, putting the cigar in the coffee cup, Green wrote BAMA.

Aloud, he said softly, "I don't see any connections between one and two. Except, where the knife went in. When it's deliberate, it's in the back. When they just explode, it's more likely to be in the front. So we got two deliberate killers. In both cases, no prints on the knife. What would Riordan say? Goddamn *shikker* is probably halfway through his first bottle of the day by now. When did I first start talking to myself? Last year? Year before? Must have been on a Sunday. The only thing is not to do it outside. But you have to do it inside. Got to hear *something*. Otherwise, you'd go bananas. No, not the fucking radio. Got to hear something that has to do with me.

"Jesus, I wonder what time she gets up on a Sunday. The kid must be up. But that doesn't mean she's up. Maybe lunch. Maybe dinner. Maybe you're a total schmuck. Put yourself in her head. Would you, the way she looks, sleep with a fat old cop? But I'll settle for the talking. It's not a violation to look at her."

Green looked at the clock. Nine-twenty. "I'm calling her about the case, right? I want to know more about Kathleen when she was at the paper. You can call any-time on public business, right?"

Green got out his notebook, went to the phone and dialed. A man's voice was on the other end.

"Hello? Hello? Who's calling?"

Sounded chipper. Why shouldn't the motherfucker sound chipper? Green hung up.

"What the hell is that?" he said to Merle Haggard, who would not turn around. "Having a guy in bed with her, and a ten-year-old kid in the next room! *Trayf!*"

Green looked at the yellow pad, looked at the phone, looked at his gun, went into the living room, got out a Billie Holiday album, found "Let's Call the Whole Thing Off," put it on and listened, nodding his head.

"Yeah. Yeah, baby, just you and me."

An hour later, in Chelsea, a thin woman, early twenties, long, straight black hair, is sitting on a stoop beside an even thinner bearded man of roughly the same age. *Bad news,* McKibbon, walking by, thought. *Both of them.*

"I saw the suitcases," she was saying, her voice hard and anxious. "I don't want any surprises."

Got to be a felony. Sam bemusedly looked straight ahead. *Well, I got probable cause for nothing. Maybe I'll read about it in the papers.* And he went on to Riordan's walk-up.

The Sunday *Times,* unopened, was on the floor by the kitchen table. Riordan, after motioning McKibbon to a chair, himself sat down heavily and poured gin into his teacup. There was no tea in sight, and the kettle looked cold.

"You remember,"—Riordan looked past Sam—"on the evening of the Resurrection, John says, 'the doors were closed in the room where the disciples were, for fear of the Jews.' And Jesus came and showed them his hands and his side. But one of the Twelve was not there."

Sam got a cup and poured himself some gin. "Yeah, I always wondered what Tom was up to that night."

"Thomas, when he was told that Jesus had come, said, 'Unless I see the holes that the nails made in his hands and can put my finger into the holes they made, and unless I can put my hand into his side, I refuse to believe.' "

McKibbon loosened his tie, pushed the cup of gin away and said brightly, "But eight days later, all the cats were together, and—"

" 'The doors were closed, but Jesus came in and stood among them.' And he spoke to Thomas: 'Put your finger here; look, here are my hands. Give me your hand; put it into my side. Doubt no longer, but believe.' And Thomas did—believe. Do you remember the rest? Do you remember what Jesus said?"

" 'You believe because you can see me. Happy are those who have not seen and yet believe.' "

Riordan looked fixedly at the wall. "It's hearsay," he finally said. "We have nothing directly from Thomas."

"It's *all* hearsay." McKibbon began to fill his pipe. "We don't even have an autopsy report. But the man took care of that. 'Happy are those who have not seen and yet believe.' Mind if I put on the water?"

"I wish I had caught that case," Riordan continued in his customary near-whisper. "He was a bunco artist, the lousy Hebrew."

"He wasn't crucified?" McKibbon looked at his pipe.

"He was in the crowd, watching."

"So who was that up there?"

Riordan looked at McKibbon and said angrily, "What the hell does that matter? There are always plenty of patsies to take a fall."

McKibbon, frowning, leaned forward. "You trying to tell me something?"

Riordan smiled thinly.

"You're trying to tell me that we believe what we want to believe." McKibbon pushed the cup away. "Even us professional disbelievers?"

"In a pinch," Riordan softly chortled.

"Lieutenant,"—McKibbon looked at the ceiling— "you are one hell of a teacher. Best I ever had anywhere. That's why I keep coming back. But could you be straight with me? What are you saying?"

Riordan drank deeply, and with relish, from his cold cup. "Consider," he said, "the easy faith that proclaims the fiddler killed the punk. And this with no physical evidence at all."

McKibbon sighed. "There were no prints on the gun that finished Tyrone. But that figures. I mean, the fiddler must at least have gone to normal school. It had to be the fiddler, Lieutenant. My God, did you ever hear of a stronger motivation?"

Riordan looked calmly at the detective. "Go back to the gospel, Sam. Let us say Jesus was in the crowd, watching. His own Hebrews called him a sorcerer. You must have busted some scam artists in your time. Get the picture?"

"You're going on assumptions," McKibbon said. "You don't know that he was in the crowd any more than you know he was up on the cross."

"Indeed, I have the disadvantage of not having been there, but had I been, I think I could have nailed him, so to speak, because I would not have been happy to simply believe. That is the point I am making, my son. There is too much simple belief in this case. Another example. Who killed Emma?"

"Tyrone."

"Why?"

"Motivation. She brought Barney down on him. Hard. Awful hard. Being part of that scene was the most important thing in the world to that punk. And she got him thrown out. She took away everything he had."

Riordan opened the refrigerator, looked at an ancient English muffin, cursed it softly and closed the door. "Insofar as that information proves to be accurate, you still have not placed Tyrone in Emma's kitchen on that night."

"Give me an alternative."

Riordan smiled. "You wouldn't say that to a defense attorney. You shouldn't say it to yourself either. You don't go forward, son, until *you* have crushed all other alternatives. Now, I am not out on this case, just as I missed the one two thousand years ago. I am just telling you to remember Thomas. He wanted to be able to put his hand into that fellow's side. Thoroughly admirable. I would have dearly loved to have had Thomas in my command."

McKibbon sighed. "Okay. Tell me more about Tyrone."

Riordan leaned across the table. "Does it make sense to you that this punk, having been so heartily and viciously punished for trying to rob the lady, would then ask for more and worse punishment by ending her life?"

McKibbon shook his head. "You're assuming Tyrone was that clear a thinker, especially right after he'd been carved up that way. He was an animal, Lieutenant, and he reacted like an animal."

"Would you like some bacon and eggs?"

"Just bacon, please, no eggs. You really think Tyrone didn't do it?"

"I am merely suggesting that *you* think. And that you walk with Thomas."

"And the fiddler?"

"Same suggestion."

"Tell me," McKibbon said, "I always thought, I guess everybody always thought, you were a practicing Catholic. I mean, really *in* the faith, not just taking out a travel insurance policy."

"Ah,"—Riordan turned the bacon over—"have I sounded blasphemous to you this morning? Could I not have been simply trying to catch your attention by unexpected means? The same sort of thing you do when you interrogate a suspect? Perfectly standard."

"Then you do believe Jesus was up there?"

The lieutenant amiably bared his teeth. "What difference does it make, what I think about him?"

"Or what he thinks about you?"

"I did not hear either of you reading me my rights."

The next morning, in a coffee shop around the corner

from the station house, Green savagely ground out his cigar in the bacon and eggs.

"Yeah," McKibbon said. "Me too."

"What you said about us having nothing real on Tyrone makes sense. If the motherfucker was alive, we'd have to let him go. It's so fucking obvious when you think about it. But I've stopped thinking. It just *figured* he went after Emma."

"Well, it didn't come to me right away, you know."

"But it did come to you."

McKibbon started to speak, stopped and then said, "You got something else on your mind than this."

"What are you," Green muttered, "some kind of detective?"

"Listen,"—McKibbon played with the coffee spoon— "I've been down that road. Remember that Abbey, the one I nearly ODed on a couple of years ago?"

"She back in Atlanta?"

"I don't know where she is." McKibbon's voice was hard and flat. "I don't want to know. Unless she's dying. I'd make that funeral anywhere. Bitch. They make you feel like shit, some of them. First one like that I knew, I was fifteen. And that's right when I stopped going to confession. What the fuck do they know? Most important thing in the world, and they don't know diddley squat about it. That's what I said to the priest. 'I'm sitting here,' I said, 'ready, oh am I ready, to sell my soul to the devil, any terms he wants, if he makes her my slave, so what the hell have I got to talk to you about? Can you make me a better deal? Man, you don't even know *what* I'm talking about.'"

"What did the priest say?" Green was intrigued.

"I don't know. I think he was asleep. I mean, what could he say? It's like talking to a deaf man about Johnny Hodges."

"What happened with you and that first one?"

"The devil never made me an offer," McKibbon said regretfully. "She slept with half the guys in school. But I was in the other half."

"Well, with Abbey, at least you lived with her for— what was it?—about a year."

"That was worse. I never had her, not for a minute. Bitch. Nothing like touching a woman, and she's not there."

There was silence. The waitress left the checks, and there was more silence.

"I'm fucking you up, partner," Green said. "I'm not functioning."

"Put your mind on the fiddler," McKibbon said soft and slow. "Don't think of anything but the fiddler. Oh, that redhead'll be moving around in your head, but stay on the fiddler. Only way to beat an obsession is with another obsession. I'll cover for you on the other stuff— Kathleen, whatever."

Green nodded. "Yeah. Maybe that's the ticket. Thanks."

"The redhead's really been giving it to you, huh?"

Green looked into the bacon and eggs with its cigar centerpiece. "Well, um, I don't know how to put this without sounding like a total *yold*, which, of course, I am."

"She dump you, just like that?"

"Well," Green squirmed, "I never even tried anything yet, you know."

McKibbon stared at him. "Wait a minute. You're tearing yourself up over some rejection that ain't ever happened? You just got bar mitzvahed or something?"

"Listen,"—Green took out a cigar—"I took her out to the Gate to hear Art Blakey, and I took her out again, and, well, I got a kind of sense that, well, I don't know what kind of sense it was, except that she sort of, maybe, liked me a little, or anyway, didn't dislike me, you know."

"But she didn't climb all over you in the taxi?"

"Come on, Sam, don't make this any harder. Anyway, I couldn't get her out of my head, and Sunday morning, well, I called her."

"Don't tell me." McKibbon, with no little effort, did not smile. "A male answered the phone. Not a little boy, a man."

"Yeah, that's right. I mean, she was under no obligation to tell me she was living with anybody, right?"

"Noah, for Christ's sake."

"Well, I knew I had no claim on her. Anyway, that's the end of that."

"End of what? Show me the beginning. For God's sake, maybe it was a relative. Maybe it was the Holy Ghost. But before you go into mourning, find out. Jesus, in another month, you'll be sucking your thumb."

"I know where it's at." Green stirred the bacon and eggs with the cigar. "Even without the guy on the phone, there was nothing could happen. What could she want with an *alter cocker?* Okay, I'm going to find Bama. What are you going to tell Randazzo?"

"You're on a lead. Getting close. And I'm going to tell him that Green's got a lot of stamina for an *alter cocker.*"

Green got up, put his hand on McKibbon's shoulder for a moment and left.

Watching his bulky partner squaring his shoulders and lifting his chin as he neared the door of the restaurant, McKibbon shook his head. *When it comes to women, the son of a bitch has as much confidence as a mole in daylight. Funny thing is, I bet she does dig him. Something that night, outside the professor's house, the way she was teasing him. Yeah. What do they call it? A* shadchen. *Yeah. Why not? If I can get her in the sack with Noah, I'll have a partner again. Shit. Nobody said a word about this in the police academy.*

14 Looking in the window of the Lone Star Café that night, the tall, lean, bearded man in the long, baggy brown coat and the gray Irish cap pulled over his eyes could see only a corner of the bandstand through the crowd. *Carl at the steel guitar, nothing on his face, like there's no connection between his face and his fingers. As if someone were playing him. There's Duncan! Jesus, they found Duncan. I thought he was driving a truck somewhere in Louisiana. Wish I could hear what he's doing on the fiddle. And that girl. Who the hell's that girl in the band?*

She was singing, but he couldn't hear her. *Goddamn crowd. Full of beer as usual. Full of themselves. Hank Williams could come back from the dead, and they wouldn't shut up for a second. God, she looks good. Made just right. Those hips. Hardly moving at all, but she doesn't have to do anything with that body. I'd hate to be Jimmy playing drums behind her. Jesus, she could mess up anybody's time. That long, black hair going down past her waist. Schoolgirl's waist. Good morning, little schoolgirl, how do you do? I been waiting a long time for you.*

That was it. The set was over. He went around the corner, into a bar and grill, ordered a beer and waited. Carl came in, grinned at the bartender.

"Triple. Fuckers tonight drive you crazy, 'less you get yourself somewhere else in your head."

When the bartender moved away, the man in the long coat stood behind Carl and said casually, "Glad you guys finally got yourselves a *good* fiddler."

"What you drinking, friend?" Carl said without turning around.

"Nothing," Bama said.

Slowly, abstractedly, Carl went into his pocket, found what he wanted and said, softly, still without turning around, "Amazing I can keep playing that thing, my fingers can't keep hold of nothing else these days." And, his hand under the bar, he dropped what was in it.

The man behind bent down to tie a shoelace, picked up the money, walked farther down the bar and ordered another beer.

Carl waited for another voice behind him, a big cop's hand digging into his shoulder. But there was nothing. He went into his pocket again, shook his head ruefully and said to the bartender, "Hey, what a damn thing. I forgot my money. Catch you after the next set?"

The bartender nodded. "Don't worry about it, man. Keep on keeping on. One triple ain't never enough for you."

"That's mighty kind of you," Carl said, seeing but ignoring the man in the long coat leaving the bar. He finished the drink, looked at the women at the bar and at the tables, making a list of those he'd like to sleep with. It was a short list, and he left.

In the dressing room, below the bandstand at the club, Carl picked up his white Stetson, lit a cigarette and asked the drummer if he could spare fifty. "Got something real good later, but she needs preparing. I'll come by your room tomorrow and give it to you."

"Just about clean me out," Jimmy said. "But with all that preparing going on, you gotta tell me about it tomorrow." He smiled. "You know, I got a funny feeling last set. It was like Bama was around. I looked, I looked real good, but I didn't see him. But hell, he wouldn't come around here."

"'Course he wouldn't," Carl said.

"Nothing at all?" Barney asked sadly. It was a little before midnight, and he sat next to Whipple in a parked car on a side street in Queens.

"Nothing." Whipple was also glum. "I tried them all. All the places he ever played. The bars he hung out in, the bars she liked. I've been to fiddle makers. He had his made special. I've been all up and down the fucking Village, all times of the day and night, because if he's after you, like you say, he's going to stay right down there. I can use some brandy."

Barney chose not to hear the request, keeping his flask in his pocket. "The Yid kid still on your mind?"

"I've been doing your business, Barney, that's all I've been doing."

Barney shifted his huge hams. "I think that kid's still on your mind. I think he's bugging the hell out of you. I think you'd be doing one hell of a lot better if your little mind was all clear. I think that boy's gotta be paid a visit."

Whipple winced. "Lay off, Barney. I beg you, lay off. You do that, and I'll be in real trouble."

"Where the hell you think you are right now? Now you hear me. I seen you track before. I never seen you miss. So it must be you fucking up now because that kid is fucking up your head. So we gonna take care of that. Right away. My boys already been doing their home-work. That little prick ain't going to say nothing no more to no police. Nothing. Including nothing about why he ain't saying no more. You going to be all clear, little fart, you dig?"

"You're not going to kill him? Jesus, they'd never let me alone, ever."

"See, see,"—Barney brought his fist down hard on Whipple's thigh—"that Yid kid has disconnected your whole head. You don't even talk like yourself no more. You can't think no more. You ain't even funny no more. Why the hell do I have to have the kid killed when I can make him an offer he can't refuse, hee, hee? Now you hear me, we're gonna take care of that kid, so all you got to be afraid of now is me. I got to get this Bama off *my* mind. I'm gonna give you three more days. You don't find him by then, they're gonna find everything but your head. We gonna stuff it and give it—anonymously, you understand—to the National Gallery of Faggots."

"Barney,"—Whipple was rubbing his thigh—"what if we've been wrong? What if the fiddler's not in the city? What if he's waiting down South somewhere until he figures you figure nothing's going to happen?"

Barney brought his face closer to Whipple's. "He's here. He wants me so bad, he can't wait much longer."

"Why are you so sure?" Whipple looked up at him.

"Because I know. I know he's gonna kill me or I'm gonna kill him. But I can't kill him if I can't find him. My boys can't find him, cops can't find him, ain't nobody can find him, but now your head is all clear, you gonna find him. And you got three days. From right now."

"You're funnin' me, Barney."

Barney patted Whipple's head. "You think those little boys are going to miss you, little fart?"

Whipple looked down at his feet, then looked directly at Barney and smiled.

"Something just went on in your sneaky head," Barney said. "Don't try nothing smart, because I got smarts you ain't smart enough to even imagine."

"Oh, I know that." Whipple took the black man's hand

and, trying to genuflect in the front seat, kissed Barney's ring finger. Quickly, he took his handkerchief and brushed it over the finger. "God, I wouldn't want you to catch anything, Barney."

Walking along, reading *The Economist* in the twilight of the next day, Adam Horowitz bumped into a short gorilla. "Jesus!" He dropped the magazine, looked again and laughed. The guy was wearing a mask. And there were two more. A tall, leering Richard Nixon and a large, round, mournful pig.

"You missed Halloween," the boy said admiringly. "Unless it's a party."

"It's a party," said Richard Nixon. "For you."

The pig and the gorilla took Adam and lifted him into a doorway. Two young men, one with his arm around the other's waist, were walking by. Both smiled. "That's what I love about the Village," one of them said. "Nobody's afraid of having *fun.*"

"You like your mama?" Richard Nixon butted Adam gently in the forehead.

"Sure. Of course I do." Adam's lips trembled.

"*We* know your mama," the pig giggled. "We know what she look like. Skinny lady, skinny hair. Can't tell where she keep her pocketbook. Smart lady. Don't wear no chains neither."

The boy looked from one mask to the other. "What do you want?" Horowitz's voice cracked.

"You got to stop talking to the po-lice," Richard Nixon said. "You say one more word to the po-lice about any single thing,"—he pulled a hunting knife from his overcoat pocket—"and your mama won't be coming home no more. She be gone. All gone. Shame. Smart lady, all gone like that."

"What police?" Adam bit his lips. "I don't know what you're talking about."

"Shee-it," the pig said. "I am surprised. *This boy playing games with us.* This boy don't give a shit about his mama."

"This boy," Richard Nixon said, "think we dumb. This boy think we don't know where he go, who he see, what he say."

"We watch you all the time," said the gorilla, "and we see you with the po-lice. Talkin' and talkin' and talkin'—"

"While his poor mama," the pig squealed, "she fading fast. Poor, poor mama."

"Help!" the boy yelled, though he saw no one nearby.

"Help!" Richard Nixon, chortling, yelled.

"Help!" chorused the pig and the gorilla, as the three of them closed in on Horowitz. Richard Nixon reached underneath the boy's coat, grabbed his balls and squeezed. Horowitz screamed and, on a signal from Richard Nixon, the three danced around the boy, with the gorilla clamping a hand on his mouth.

"Nobody coming," said the pig.

"Somebody could be watching from a window," Richard Nixon said. "This way, it look like we all be on something. All right, boy, you listenin'?"

Horowitz nodded, tears coming down his cheeks.

"One word—" Richard Nixon was breathing into his face. "One fucking word to that nigger detective, or any of the rest of those cocksuckers, and your mama going to be cut up fifteen different ways. We know every move she make. Fourteenth floor, four-four-four Madison, right? Right. One thirty-two West seven-six, that's where her sister be, right? Right. And every Sunday morning, ten o'clock, Russ and daugh-ters, One seventy-nine East Houston, for that fine Nova Scoatchia and cream cheese, right? Right. We find her anytime we want to. And you be the murderer—'cause you couldn't keep your fuckin' mouth shut. People gonna talk about you all your days. There's the boy that killed his mama 'cause he couldn't keep his fuckin' mouth shut."

"Tell me, boy,"—Richard Nixon butted Horowitz in the forehead again, harder—"you think we foolin'?"

Adam shook his head. "No," he whispered.

"You want to keep your mama," the gorilla said, "keep your fuckin' mouth *shut.*"

With Richard Nixon in the lead, followed by the pig and the gorilla, the partygoers left the boy in the doorway. As they turned the corner, Horowitz heard Nixon howling, and he saw the pig and the gorilla turning somersaults.

15 To be shunned by a dog. Green, the evening of the following day, was shaking his head as he filled the dish with dog food. Merle Haggard, under the sink, looked stonily into the living room. The slash in his throat had healed, but the scar was still mean and red.

"I know the routine, you bastard," Green muttered. "I got to be in the bedroom, where you can't see me, before you'll eat. That way it didn't come from me. Motherfucker. I took you in to be sure you'd be all right, and you come on like *I'm* the intruder. First time in my life I've ever locked the bedroom door when I go to bed. You're not going to get the jump on me, you fiend."

Merle Haggard gave no sign of hearing, but his ears shot up when the phone rang.

"Green here."

"Hi, it's Shannon. Look, could I come see you? I've been taken off the story, but I'm doing it on my own. I'm going to show those creeps."

"Why did they take you off?" Green kept his voice neutral.

"They said I sounded like I was doing PR for the Department. Like, why wasn't Ginsburg brought in? Who's his rabbi? Like that. Assholes!"

Green frowned. "Then why go to a police source?"

"Because I don't think you lie, damn it. And I don't think there's anything funny going on. I think you guys are doing what you can."

"Well," Green smiled, "how can I say no to a tribute? Where should I meet you?"

"I can come over there if you'll tell me where there is."

"Two forty-five West One hundred seventh, corner of Broadway. Five-C."

"Okeydoke. See you."

Green rushed through the living room, picking up papers, magazines and a bottle of scotch off the floor, putting the scotch on the bar and dumping the papers and magazines into the bedroom closet. In the kitchen, he looked at the dishes piled precariously in the sink, sighed, grabbed a shopping bag, stacked the dishes inside and put the bag in the bedroom closet. Wiping off the kitchen table, he looked at Merle Haggard. "You too," he said and pointed peremptorily toward the bedroom. The dog did not move, but when Green went into the hallway to throw the garbage in the incinerator, Merle Haggard slowly, off-handedly, meandered into the bedroom and went under the bed.

Having made the bed, or rather having hidden the crumpled sheets under a blanket, Green looked at the clothes on the floor and on the chair. "Hell," he said, "it's a waste of time. This is the one place she won't go anywhere near." Still, he picked up all the clothes and shoved them into the closet.

In the living room, Green poured himself some scotch, then walked into the kitchen and looked out the window. Seeing no sign of the press, he went back and poured himself another drink.

Green had been pacing near the front door when the bell rang. He had intended to count a few beats before he opened the door, but he grabbed the knob on the first ring.

"Let me take your coat," he said, surprised, as always, that she was taller than he had remembered.

"Thanks," Shannon said, her hair just as soft as he had remembered, her face even more cheerful and her ass every bit as dangerous.

"Drink?" Green asked.

"Yeah. Very light scotch and water."

He made it, along with another for himself.

"Say,"—she took out a notebook—"did I ever tell you about my brother, used to work out of the Thirteenth Precinct?"

"You said you'd had a cop in the family."

"Yeah, well, he's an investigator now for the Suffolk County DA's office. He stays over sometimes when he's in the city."

"And?"

"Oh, come on, I can't play games. He was the guy who answered when you called, you schmuck."

Green could not suppress a very large grin. "How do you know I called?" He tried to be serious again.

"Confidential source. You may subpoena me, but it will do you no good."

"I don't have to subpoena anybody. Goddamn McKibbon thinks he's a *shadchen.*"

"Just the word he used. Oops!" She giggled. "Well, he certainly meant no harm."

"He didn't do any either. Why did you want me to know?"

"Oh God. Okay,"—she took out a pen—"let's get to the case."

"Later." Green stood up, came over to her, touched her hair, drew her up and put his arms around her.

"Hey!" she said, "I'm not fragile, but on the other hand, I got ribs that can crack."

In the bedroom, as she took off her dress, Shannon saw

a large snout emerging from under the bed and screamed. Merle Haggard, his huge face full of melancholy, looked directly at her.

"Out!" Green, one stocking on, one stocking off, roared. But the dog did not move.

"That must be Bama's," Shannon Leahy said, leaning down.

"Stay away, you don't know what that monster will do!"

"I know what he wants." She tickled Merle Haggard under his devil's ears, patted his head, rubbed his back and then his belly. The dog did not take his eyes off her.

"Okay," Green said, feeling foolish with nothing on but a sock and wholly bereft of authority, *"you* tell him to get the hell out."

She knelt down and whispered into Merle Haggard's ear, "In the kitchen."

Merle Haggard left. Green closed the door and removed the remaining sock while Shannon Leahy was laughing so hard she was doubled over. The detective straightened her up and then gently eased her down on the bed.

Barney, around seven the next morning, was looking out the window of his brownstone on Twelfth Street near Fifth Avenue. "Well, the dude ain't gonna deliver. That Whipple only got another day. We got to go another way, Arthur."

The tall beige man with the elegant mustache nodded. "When do we remove the little dude?" Barney's general manager asked.

"No hurry. Maybe he'll scare himself to death—save us the trouble."

"He could turn," Arthur said.

"Not with what they've got on him, or what he thinks

they've got on him." Barney kept looking out the window.

"He could trade. He knows something of what we do."

"Nah, he killed a woman, man; he can't trade us for that."

"Nonetheless, I would feel better with him gone." Arthur checked his mustache in the mirror. "Why, if I may ask, are you waiting?"

"First things first," Barney said. "I got no more patience. Gotta make the fiddler find me, get it over with. I am going to be seen again, Arthur, all over the fucking place."

"In all the old familiar places," Arthur gently sang as he carefully filled a meerschaum pipe with tobacco. "The fiddler, he wants to take you that bad, he will take you in the open."

"No, he won't. He wants me to die slow, with him getting off at each croak. He couldn't stand for it to be all over in a second. No, he wants to get me all to himself, some place inside, some quiet place."

"Here?" Arthur looked at Barney. "You intend to lead him here? Not a bad idea. Only you and I know about this place."

"Couldn't be better, could it?" Barney turned back into the living room. "He follows me here, but he don't know who's inside, so he cases the place for a day or two, and at night. And he gonna find it's just me. 'Cause you won't be anywhere around. You know what I mean. You won't be anywhere he can see. Then he gonna make his move."

"Just the two of us are going to take him?"

"Shit, Arthur, what do we need an army for? Just keep it to ourselves."

At that hour, in the squad room, Randazzo was glaring

at McKibbon as he strode by. "Too cold out for you?"

"I'm going, Lieutenant. I want to see that kid again, but I want to get him on the way to school, about forty minutes from now. And I spent most of yesterday afternoon talking to the professor. Nothing new there."

"Going or staying doesn't seem to make much difference," Randazzo said sourly. "I don't hear nothing from your partner either. That fucking fiddler's scored once, now he's loading up again for Barney."

"I don't think Bama killed Tyrone," McKibbon said.

"Think? What good does think do me? You got another suspect?"

"My gut says Barney got the kid."

"Terrific," Randazzo said. "Why don't you send your gut out to bring him in?"

"I don't have anything hard yet."

"You know,"—Randazzo stood at the door of his office —"if you guys got paid on your clearance rate these days, you'd have to go on welfare." And going in, he banged the door behind him.

"Son of a bitch is right," McKibbon said as the phone rang.

"Hey,"—the normally low and even voice had taken on the resonance of a Heldentenor, except that he was a baritone—"I owe you one! Boy, do I owe you one."

"That's the opening I need, Noah," McKibbon said. "Listen, since I got a rooting interest in this now, I'm going to give you some advice. I never take it myself, that's how I know it's good, being a many-time loser in these matters. You hear me?"

"Go ahead," said Green.

"I know how long it's been, but let her breathe some. Don't try to own her, you know. That's all."

"I don't know what the hell you're talking about. I

mean, I do know, but this thing with me and Shannon's mutual, Sam. It's miraculous, but it's mutual."

"Okay. *Mazel tov*, my man. Doing any business?"

"That fiddler is smarter than I thought. It's like I just started looking. Or maybe he did go home to throw us all off, especially Barney."

"Of course, he wouldn't go *home* down there," McKibbon said.

"Yeah. But he could be holed up in Georgia or Tennessee or Texas, for all I know. He's played all through there." Green paused. "No, Sam. I'm just whistling Dixie. He didn't go South. He couldn't stand not being here. I got to keep on going over the same ground again. I got to lean on those musicians again. He probably changed himself some. Dyed his hair, grew a beard, something. But sooner or later, he's got to go to the music. To the musicians. Well, thank you again. And hey, when you walk up the aisle, see if you can keep your gun from showing."

"I'll let Riordan hold it," McKibbon said.

"Fuck you, pal."

McKibbon hung up the phone and was putting on his coat when the phone on Green's desk rang.

"Detective Green, he's there?"

"No, Domingo, this is Sam."

"Oh, you're not supposed to be talking to me, right?" Domingo snickered.

"Lot of things I'm not supposed to do, but I lose track. Noah's going to be hard to reach, so tell me, and I'll get it to him."

"Okay." Domingo spoke fast. "Barney's back on the scene. In the park, in Blimpie's, on Sheridan Square. Like he's a parade, man, all by himself. That's all."

"Any idea why he's showing himself?" McKibbon asked.

"I don't go in for, what you call 'em, analysis. I just bring the news."

"Any news about those *bodega* killings, or about who took off Stubblefield?"

"Have a nice day, Sam. And a long life to us all."

"Thanks," McKibbon said. "From your lips to God's ear." He hung up the phone and, rubbing his pipe, muttered, "Did Barney bury the fiddler? Now, where the hell can I find Noah? Oh yeah." McKibbon dialed the *Journal,* left the news with Shannon Leahy and went downtown.

A half hour later, McKibbon was watching the boy walking fast toward the bus stop and then, with long strides, the detective caught up with him.

Adam Horowitz put his hand over his mouth when he saw the detective, shook his head from side to side and moved down the street.

Again, McKibbon caught up with him. "You're going to be late for school, you keep playing hide and seek."

The boy just kept shaking his head.

"You had a visitor?"

Horowitz, looking down at the ground, did not answer.

"Whipple? The guy in the candy store?"

The boy shook his head hard, very hard.

"Had to be somebody. Or somebodies. They said if you talk to me, that's the end of you, right?"

No answer.

"They said they're gonna get your mother?"

The look in the boy's eyes gave McKibbon his answer.

"Listen, Adam, you'll never have a clearer choice in your whole life. You can deal with these animals whose word isn't worth shit, or you can deal with me. Which way you figure your mother's going to be safe? You hear me? You keep dealing with them, she's a corpse for sure. And then you."

The boy was looking down and would not lift his eyes.

"Okay," McKibbon said softly. "Then I'm going to have to talk to your mother."

McKibbon saw the tears for just a second as the boy broke and ran. There was no point going after him yet. *The kid'll have a miserable day at school, and I'll be waiting for him when he comes out.*

The detective looked around to see if there had been any interested onlookers. None. But even if there had been, behind a window, the kid hadn't said a mumbling word. So there was time. *Smart dumb kid.*

McKibbon moved toward Sheridan Square. *I never figured Crocker would be that gross. But who did he send to work over the kid? The faggot's a loner. But he does deal with Barney. Could be Barney's boys who scared the shit out of the kid. But where the hell's the connection? Why should Barney get himself involved in the Ginsburg case? What does he owe Crocker? First things first. I got to see the kid's mother, who's going to give me a lot of hell, which she should, for getting her boy into this.*

He stopped at the corner. *Does any of this connect with Emma? No, I'm not going to go see Riordan again. I'm all grown up. I get paid to figure out all this shit by myself.*

Late that morning, Carl opened the door of his hotel room, and was not surprised.

"You expecting anybody?" said the tall, lean, bearded man.

"Nope. Wasn't that kind of risky the other night?"

"Yeah, maybe." Bama took off his coat and sat down on the edge of a chair. "I got mugged the night before so I was real short. I thank you." He handed Carl five ten-dollar bills.

"Hey, no damn hurry."

"That's all right. You know, a guy doesn't have to work at all in this town. You find the right places, and if you're white, polite—and southern, they do take to the way we talk—you can make out mooching. Most of the time."

"Where do you sleep, Bama?"

"Different places. No place long enough for anybody to remember me. If I have a string of dead days, I sleep with the rummies at one of the chicken coops on the Bowery. I used to grab some sleep on the subway once in a while, but not since I got mugged. Can't figure out why I didn't get it down there before. Jesus, Carl, you bring a gorilla down there and he wouldn't have a chance. They'd go right for his coat. And,"—Bama settled back into the chair—"some nights, I treat myself to a nice crummy room like this one."

Carl went into the bedroom and came back with a bottle of bourbon and glasses. Bama looked yearningly at the bottle but put up his hand. "After being dry so long, I won't be able to stop. So, thanks, but not until I get the job done."

"Any idea when that'll be?"

"Barney's not hiding anymore," the fiddler said. "That means he wants me to come to him. I got him real nervous. I feel like one of them hounds my daddy had. They never let nothing get away. It's a great feeling, Carl. And the cops, *they* want me to come to him too. So I'm going to accommodate everybody. It's almost over, Carl."

"That Jew cop's been around."

Bama smiled. "Noah? Yeah, I saw him a couple of times on the street, but before he saw me. He been giving you guys a hard time?"

"He's trying. I'd like to see him one last time before I leave this place."

Bama looked at him. "You don't like no Jews at all, do you?"

"That's right." Carl refilled his glass. "You know who owns that place we been playing? Getting rich off McClinton, Merle, even Ernest Tubb been there. That's right. A Jew. Makes me sick. Well, you got other things on your mind. Bama, it's none of my business, but why are you after that guy Barney so bad? It was that nigger kid that—"

"No, it wasn't," Bama said coolly.

"Then why did you—"

"I didn't. I ain't killed nobody yet, Carl."

The steel-guitar player rubbed his chin and reached out for the glass. "Well, knowing you, you got to know what you're doing. That Barney ain't got a chance."

Bama laughed. "How's Merle?"

"The cop's got him. Probably circumcised him."

"Listen, Carl, when he's not chasing me, that cop is a friend of mine, okay?"

Carl nodded and poured himself some bourbon.

"Hey," Bama said, "you got any Bill Monroe?"

Carl got up, went through a pile of albums on the floor, picked one out and put on "Roll in My Sweet Baby's Arms."

The fiddler grinned all the way through. "No more," he said when it was over. "The music's like the bourbon. But I figured I could handle one by Bill. You remember what he used to say, after the show, when we were opening for him on that tour?"

"What in particular?" Carl was puzzled.

"I learned it. I learned what he said word for word." The fiddler took a breath. " 'Let them fine, high tones ring out. Don't flowery it up too much, boy; you got to love that melody and work at it so's the peoples will love it the same way. You got to chase the melody like a foxhound.'"

Carl nodded. "As good as scripture."

"And he wasn't just talking about music," Bama said. "That's the way to live a life."

"Amen."

"Way to end one too."

"Bama, you need anything?"

"I might, Carl. I might need you."

"I'm ready. Yes, sir, I'm always ready. And I specially like it when I don't know what it's gonna be."

16 Early that afternoon, in an Italian restaurant in the Village that had been unreservedly recommended by Lieutenant Randazzo, Shannon Leahy was beaming at Detective Green.

"Would you want another kid?" Green seemed to be speaking to Shannon's glass of wine.

"For Christmas?" She put her hand on his.

"What I was thinking, actually,"—Green stopped as the waiter brought their antipastos—"is that *I* sure would. But if we did, Jesus, I'd be a real old man when he was sixteen. What kind of father is that?"

"Noah, there are a hell of a lot of rotten fathers in their thirties."

"Yeah, but what could I do with the boy?"

"Oh," she said, "I've seen guys in wheelchairs at the ball game."

"It wouldn't be right," Green said gloomily.

"You forget, but, of course, you haven't even realized it yet, that you've got, or at least he'll be living with you, a ten-year-old."

"Yeah, that's true."

She smiled. "Yeah, that's true, just like the income-tax form is true, and the flu is true, but you didn't ask for them. I know. He's not *yours*. Well, since you really haven't thought about what comes with me, maybe you ought to think some more about the whole thing."

Green looked at her in terror.

"Hey,"—Shannon leaned over and smoothed his hair —"I'm just teasing. I'd like another kid, and I think whatever time he—I don't know why we're both so sure it's going to be a he—whatever time he has with both of us will be good time. So what the hell, Noah? Besides, look at Strom Thurmond. He wasn't a father until he was nearly seventy. And then he sired two more."

"I'm not a southern rooster," Green growled, "and I'm not a senator. I'm an overweight, brooding Jew who smokes too much."

"And is back on the sauce," she smiled.

"That's a collector's item—sauce."

"I'm full of anachronisms—part of me charm."

Green squeezed her fingers. "Anyway, booze is good for you. Good for the circulation."

"Yeah, that's what all the *shikkers* say. Don't worry about the kid, Noah. We'll know if it's right."

"Emma sure wanted her kid." Green finished his scotch and water. "You know, I think I agree with Sam. Tyrone didn't kill Emma. Then who? Barney? If it's Barney, he didn't do it himself. That's not the way he operates. It's never been. He'd order it done. Okay, let's back up. It could have been Tyrone. On orders. So, after Emma got it, then Barney ordered Tyrone killed to get rid of the only link between Barney and Emma's murder. Most probable executioner of Tyrone is Arthur, if that's the way it went.

"But why?" Green signaled for another drink. "Barney never does anything that isn't in his self-interest. That's a man who's constantly screening his impulses, otherwise we'd have had him long ago. Hell, if he'd gone legit, Barney would have fit in, way up high, in some bank or oil company. And not through affirmative action either. But there was no way Emma was any kind of obstacle or threat to Barney. So why? It makes no sense."

"Wouldn't it make sense," Shannon Leahy said, "to put Barney in protective custody? Whether or not Barney murdered Emma, Bama's going to kill him. Or Barney's going to kill Bama."

"How long could we keep him? Anyway, this has got to come to an end, so we need Barney out there. But I think I finally talked Randazzo into having Barney tailed around the clock. We'll keep the motherfucker from getting killed, and save Bama too."

"Why didn't you put a tail on Barney before?"

Green shook his head. "Because the son of a bitch is uncanny. He says he can smell a cop a mile away, and I believe it from what's happened in the past. But I didn't want him disappearing again now, and these are our two best shadows that Randazzo will put on him. They'll stick to him."

"And if he shakes them?" Shannon asked.

"They can't fit into their old uniforms. I don't think they want to buy new ones."

As McKibbon had expected, Adam Horowitz was the first kid out the door as school broke a couple of hours later. Watching from the vestibule of an old townhouse, McKibbon grinned as the boy looked anxiously, then frantically, around. As the detective walked out into the street, the boy gave a visible sigh of relief and ran up to him.

"I *knew* you'd be here," Horowitz said.

"I see the cat gave you back your tongue."

"You were right. To put my mother's life in their hands— Jesus, how stupid can you get?"

"So,"—McKibbon started walking, the boy coming along—"tell me about your visitors."

The boy described the meeting, the masks, the threats.

"Their hands, their hair?" McKibbon spoke slowly. "What color?"

"Uh, black."

"Did they say anything about our friend in the candy store, or about Mrs. Ginsburg?"

"No. But it had to be him they were talking about. I mean, they knew I'd talked to you. They mentioned you."

"In fear and trembling, I trust."

"They—uh—said—uh—nigger detective."

"They are badly brought up," McKibbon said. "We are supposed to use that terminology only among our own. I bet your mother never says 'kike' in ecumenical company but sometimes, in the bosom of the family, no other word will do, right?"

The boy shook his head. "No, sometimes she says it outside the house. But her parents were German Jews, you see."

McKibbon smiled. "Dicty is as dicty does."

"Huh?"

"Never mind. Now, figuring that your *Yiddisher kop* would soon be operating again, I did a little anticipating. On the assumption that your visitors might belong to a guy named Barney—"

"Barney who?"

"I'll fill you in on him later, but for some reason he seems to be protecting this faggot you saw with Kathleen Ginsburg."

"I'm not sure it was him, I told you."

"Who asked you? I got word to this Barney that the masks were put on so sloppily that you were able to match those boys with some mug shots, and I can tie every single one of those boys to him."

154

"But I have no idea what they look like. Their faces, I mean."

"And I made it very, very clear to this Barney,"— McKibbon went on as if he had not heard the boy—"that this is a very big case for us and that if anything happens to our key witness, or any relative of his, we will come down on this Barney so hard even his mama couldn't recognize the pieces when we got through. He got the message."

The boy looked up at McKibbon. "Are you sure he's going to leave my mother and me alone?"

"No. But I almost could be sure because the bastard has so much deep trouble of his own right now that he can do without the faggot adding to it. I don't think Barney had anything to do with the Ginsburg murder. Whatever's going on between him and our mutual friend is something else. Anyway, I've got a feeling everything's going to blow pretty soon. However, I'm not taking any chances. I want you to get your assignments for the next two weeks. Think you can catch up later on the class work?"

"What I really need, I can get somebody to tape for me," Adam said.

"And your mother, I've talked to her, she's going to take a vacation."

"Where are we going?"

"Not far,"—McKibbon patted the boy on the shoulder —"but it'll be safe. Yonkers."

"Yonkers?"

"See, who'd ever think of Yonkers? Anyway, you won't be alone."

"One thing," the boy frowned. "What you said about me recognizing those guys in the masks and about me being sure it was the faggot on the street that night, that's what the CIA calls disinformation. I mean, is it right to do that?"

"Would you rather I hadn't?" McKibbon smiled.

"But is it right? Okay, the other side lies all the time, but should cops lie?"

"Ask your mama."

17 The morning that Whipple's three days were up, it was raining hard, and he was grateful. *They're not going to get soaked to kill a man when they can wait and do it dry.* Still, he put on three bulky sweaters, a new fake-fur coat (he never wore any kind of fur, fake or not), a new thick scarf that covered chin and mouth and a new watch cap (also not his style).

To his acute disappointment, there were no cabs, so Whipple walked quickly down Christopher Street toward the subway at Sheridan Square. As he neared the entrance, a tall, thin man in a gray sweat shirt, white running pants and blue sneakers—holding a small black umbrella—jogged past and grinned at him.

"A lovely coat, Crocker," Arthur sang in the rain. "Hong Kong?"

Whipple rushed down the stairs and out of sight. Barney's general manager shook his head. "The poor faggot does not know he has a reprieve. Sort of a reprieve." And whistling "Miss Brown to You," Arthur flowed on.

At the 13th Precinct, Whipple ran up to the desk sergeant and asked for Randazzo.

"Who shall I say is calling?" The sergeant looked down at the slight man shaking, no doubt, from the cold rain.

"I'd rather not use a name." The voice was muffled by the scarf. "It'll be worth his time. Listen,"—he looked pleadingly at the sergeant—"it's a matter of life and death. It really is. And more than one death is involved."

The sergeant nodded. "You picked the right precinct. We do wholesale as well as retail. I'll let the lieutenant know you're here."

In Lieutenant Randazzo's office a few minutes later were the lieutenant himself, Green, McKibbon and an exceedingly pale Crocker Whipple.

"You got something on your mind?" Randazzo asked Whipple as he moved the jar of sour balls far out of Whipple's reach. ("Can you imagine the germs he'd put in there?" the lieutenant later told Green. "I mean the *kinds* of germs.")

Whipple, down to a beige sweater and brown corduroy pants, said tonelessly, "There's a contract out for me. It's Barney."

"A lot of people come in here saying somebody's going to kill them," said Randazzo. "Sometimes they get the word from the radio some CIA dentist put in their molars. You get both FM and AM, Whipple?"

Whipple started going through his pockets. McKibbon walked out of the room, came back with a pack of cigarettes and tossed them at Whipple.

"Keep them," Randazzo volunteered. "How do we know Barney let out a contract on you?"

"I didn't mean contract," said Whipple. "It's in-house. That Arthur."

"But how do we *know?*"Randazzo stared at him. "Just because you say so? Maybe you had a fight, a lover's quarrel or something, and you want to get Barney into trouble."

Whipple looked at Green. "You know me, Noah. You know when I'm telling the truth."

"Help me out a little." Green dug into the lieutenant's jar of sour balls. "Why does he want to kill you?"

"He's afraid," Whipple said. "He's afraid of the fiddler. He hired me to track him down, and I couldn't. God knows I tried, but that fucking Bama's the invisible man. Barney gave me a deadline. Literally. He wanted to be sure I was highly motivated. If I came up dry, I'd wind up in your file." Whipple looked at Randazzo.

"What good does it do Barney to get rid of you?" McKibbon asked coldly.

"It was around that Barney made that promise to me and to himself." Whipple was having trouble lighting his cigarette. "So he's got to do it. Barney never backs down once people are watching. He's Mr. Macho of all time."

"Well," Randazzo said, "supposing this is not just a bad dream you are having. What can we do for you? I could show you some karate."

"Listen—" Whipple gave up on the cigarette. "I can tell you a lot about Barney's operations. Not all of them, but a lot. The sex thing, and some of the drug business. Even you guys would be surprised at who some of the customers are in the sex thing. And what they bought."

"Nothing surprises me," Randazzo said matter-of-factly. "A lot of things disgust me, but I haven't been surprised for years."

"Just wait," Whipple smiled briefly. "And payoffs. Barney was a lot better connected than you can imagine. Including," he looked at Randazzo, "in this precinct."

"How'd you find out all this?" McKibbon said softly. "You weren't that tight with Barney."

"Nobody is," Whipple said, "not even Arthur. But I dealt with him. I dealt in bodies, and the bodies told me things, which led to my figuring some other things out and, then, very quietly, confirming them. I've always figured, being a one-man shop, that the best way to survive was to collect as much information as I could about anybody who might do me any harm. Barney, being Barney, was very high on that list."

"The drug end," said McKibbon, "how did you get information about that?"

"When the time comes,"—Whipple looked at him—"you'll know."

Randazzo grabbed some sour balls. "When will the time come?"

"I need to be safe." Whipple looked around the room.

"If you were a material witness," Green said slowly, "and if the DA agrees, we could hole you up at a hotel. On the other hand, it may be something for the Feds—the drug part of it anyway." He looked at Randazzo.

"No problem." The lieutenant stared at Whipple. "Barney didn't grow all those drugs in his backyard. Interstate, intercountry, what the hell? We can bring in the DEA, and they'll hole you up. They can afford better accommodations than we can."

"Everybody goes first class in the Drug Enforcement Agency," McKibbon grinned. *"Everybody."*

"Enough," Randazzo said. "Even if he knows what you're talking about, you shouldn't be talking about it in front of him."

"Everybody knows," Whipple said. "DEA is full of shit, every which way that means. Anyway, I certainly don't want any of that 'new identity' crap. All I need is some time to get myself together and figure out what next. So I'd rather stay with you guys."

"We are profoundly touched." Randazzo hungrily eyed the cigar that Green was about to light. "And you know, with an identity like yours, I don't blame you for not wanting to change it. Except maybe for a hyena's."

"If I turned,"—Whipple looked at Green—"what kind of deal do you think I'd get? I mean, if I have to do time, I might as well go out on that street right now and get killed instead of waiting for one of Barney's boys to take me off inside."

"Who's keeping you?" Randazzo snapped. "You're not in custody. You want to walk, walk."

"We can't give you any guarantee," Green said. "We can't give you any promises, direct or implied. That's all up to the DA. But—"

"But,"—Randazzo was talking to the wall—"my guess, speaking as a private person, in no way in my official capacity, is that if you produce what you say you're going to produce, the benefit to the community of cleaning up that fucking cesspool will be such as to lead the DA to give you some consideration. You understand what I'm saying?"

"Yeah," said Whipple. "You're covering yourself. I need something more specific than that."

"Hey, buddy,"—Randazzo rose and stood in front of Whipple—"what are you dealing from? You got a hand in which there is nothing on the cards. They're all blanks. That's why you're here. So don't go shitting me with you need something more specific. The only alternative you got is to walk out that fucking door. I told you, you want to walk, walk. And we'll sweep you off some vacant lot in, oh, five or six hours. Of course, we may never find you at all. In which case, we could put up a little plaque in your favorite urinal."

"Homophobes are afraid of something," Whipple said, "and it's not us."

"No shit," Randazzo roared. "You found me out. Have you got a treat coming, Mary!"

"Just going by what you say,"—McKibbon shifted his chair so he could see Whipple past Randazzo's booming body—"if this is anywhere near that big an operation, and if you really have the stuff, I wouldn't worry too much about doing time for any business you've been doing with Barney. Again, like the lieutenant, no promises. I'm just speculating, and I'm doing it unofficially.

But you've got a much bigger problem than your deals with Barney."

"Yesssss." Randazzo went back to his desk. "There is a problem about a corpse. Used to be someone called Kathleen Ginsburg."

"This stuff about Barney is big," Whipple began.

"We don't run no bargain sales here!" Randazzo yelled. "One thing is one thing, and another thing is another thing. Now, wait. Let me make this perfectly clear since this new and entirely different subject is looming before us. I am not one of those law-enforcement people who keeps complaining that the Supreme Court keeps putting handcuffs on the peace forces and takes them off the criminal forces. Every night I pray for the health of the Court because with such things as they gave us like *Miranda,* my boys had to stop fucking around. They had to produce solid cases. And you know something else? I've learned how to stay ahead of the Court. So when they come down with something new to goose due process in the ass, my boys are already doing it.

"Now, here you are, Whipple. You came in by yourself. We didn't even make a reservation for you. And ever since you've been here, has anybody said you could not walk out that door if you wanted to walk out that door?"

"Quite the opposite," Whipple said dryly.

"Attaboy, you're thinking clear. Now, if it is about to come into your mind to say anything about this corpse who used to be someone called Kathleen Ginsburg, I want you to know, right now, what your rights are. I don't *have* to give them to you because this is a voluntary situation, but in honor of the Constitution of the United States and those nine fucking farts, I'm going to give them to you anyway."

"I know my rights," Whipple said.

"Shut up!" Randazzo bellowed. "Have some respect for the Constitution!" He stood again, took a plastic-covered card from his inside coat pocket and, putting one hand over his heart, the lieutenant instructed Crocker Whipple:

"You have the right to remain silent. From this moment on.

"Anything you say can and will be used against you in a court of law.

"You have the right to talk to a lawyer and have him present with you while you are being questioned.

"If you cannot afford to hire a lawyer, one will be appointed to represent you before any questioning if you wish one.

"Now, do you want me to do it again slow?"

"No, thanks," Whipple said.

"You want it in Spanish? Sicilian? French? The French'll sound like Italian, but it's really French."

Whipple remained silent.

"You want a lawyer?" Randazzo asked.

Whipple straightened up in his chair. "I have nothing to say to you or a lawyer about that. And if you had something on me, you'd really have reason to read me my rights because I'd be in custody."

"Mr. Whipple,"—Randazzo gestured toward the door —"you are free to go. Indeed, our business being over, and our quarters being cramped, and our time being unfortunately limited due to the press of all our other business, I must insist that you leave us."

Whipple grabbed the edge of the chair, stiffened and screamed at Randazzo, "You're telling me to go out and get killed because I won't confess to something I didn't do! That's like Russia! Are you guys,"—he turned frantically to Green and then to McKibbon—"going to let this happen? Are you just going to let me get killed out there?"

"Sam," Green said, "is Tommy Flanagan still at Bradley's?"

"Two more nights." McKibbon lighted his pipe. "Got a hell of a good bass player too. George Mraz. A Czech, can you believe that?"

"The one I miss," Green said, "is Scott LaFaro. You ever hear him?"

"Great chops,"—McKibbon scratched his nose—"but no soul, not really. Now this Mraz, he's got both."

"You guys got to take me down to one of those places," said Randazzo. "Maybe I've been missing something. Do you think I'm too old to get with it?"

"Aw, Lieutenant," said McKibbon, "what a question."

"You'd really make me leave?" Whipple was shaking his head. "Christ, look at the stuff I'm giving you."

"If I had the choice,"—Randazzo was talking to McKibbon and Green—"between sending away a big piece of shit and all his little pieces of shit, foul as they are, and clearing a murder case that has the mayor and the commissioner treating me like I got terrible bad breath, which would I do?"

"Lieutenant," Green said, "why don't Mr. Whipple and I go into an empty office and chat a bit?"

Randazzo shrugged. McKibbon looked at his watch. "I got eyes for some pastrami," he said. "Anybody want anything?"

The other three shook their heads. "How about some coffee?" Green asked Whipple. "No, wait, you like Dry Sack, right? Pick up a couple of bottles, Sam."

"You sure Dry Sack is good enough?" Randazzo muttered.

"How's Connie doing?" Green sat down heavily at the

desk, loosened his tie and looked rather yearningly at the phone.

"It's nice and quiet down there," Whipple said. "Almost pastoral. She's got a new policy. You raise your voice longer than ten seconds and you're out. She even changed the music. Took one of those string quartets off the street."

"Average age must be up," Green took out a cigar.

"No. The regulars seem to like it. I like it. Very calming. Connie says you and her are even, whatever that means."

"That's right. Clean slate."

Whipple leaned forward. "You're really not going to let Randazzo just throw me out there?"

"I'm just a hired hand, Crocker."

Whipple put up his jacket collar and rubbed his hands. "You guys saving money for the city?"

"The lieutenant says people catch colds because they get too hot inside and then go out and catch a chill. The lieutenant says that since he's kept the temperature down here, he's saved hundreds, thousands, of manhours that used to be lost to colds, flu, whatever. He has the precise, up-to-date figures if you want to ask him. Crocker, let me give you some advice. I'm not questioning you about anything, you understand?"

Whipple said nothing.

"It is one thing,"—Green looked at the ash on his cigar—"to have a pretty good criminal lawyer, if you should ever need one; but if you've got the bread, and I bet you got a nice stash somewhere, you got the pick of the cream. Somebody in Raymond Brown's league. Or Bill Leibowitz. You know the names?"

"I know the names. By repute."

"Or Mike Steinberg. That is some counselor! Like a mad dog. But with brains. Did you see what he did last month? He got that cop off, the Irish cop who killed the two Puerto Ricans in that after-hours joint on the West Side. Not only were they unarmed, but both were shot in the back."

"I read the story."

"Self-defense. And the jury bought it."

"That may work with a cop," Whipple said, "but not with a civilian. Especially not with someone gay. Not even Steinberg could pull that one off."

"Stay with me. You talk about gays. People in this town—or rather, people in the one and only borough of Manhattan—are pretty liberal when it comes to anything consensual, right? Whatever folks want to do in their own bedrooms or, for that matter, even in public toilets, so long as they keep their hands on each other and don't go groping straight citizens who've come in to do something else. I mean, it's not worth bothering about. The police got more important things to do, right?"

Whipple was impassive.

"But as liberal as a Manhattan jury might be, they don't like predators. I'll give you a hypothetical, like the lawyers say. There's this bull dyke. Mean. Somebody she wants to grab says no thanks; the dyke belts the shit out of her. Okay, so one night, this diesel really gets out of line. She goes after a whore, one of the AC/DC types, but the whore's pimp gets very salty because it's on his time. There is a dispute, ending up in one dead bull dyke."

Green moved his chair closer to Whipple as he continued. "Pimp goes on trial, represented by Mike Steinberg. Jurors don't like pimps, but they don't like lesbians more because they do not understand lesbians at all. And jurors especially do not like bull dykes who beat up on women, even if those women are lesbians."

"How could Steinberg bring that into evidence?" Whipple asked. "The past history of her having beat up women? She's the goddamn victim, for Christ's sake. Or was."

"Ah," Green said, "but if Steinberg is arguing self-defense, he can introduce evidence of the violent character of the initial aggressor. In this case, the dyke, even if she wound up losing the fight. Of course, the prosecution can then introduce evidence of what a thoroughly rotten son of a bitch the pimp is, but that's not news. The main thing is to get the jury to see how uncontrollably violent this dyke was.

"So, having set up the dyke, so to speak, Steinberg puts the pimp on the stand. The pimp is very well rehearsed, and he presents a very vivid account of what happened that night. He is speaking to the dyke about not coming around and pawing his property during office hours. He is speaking firmly, but he has not raised a hand. All of a sudden the dyke—who is one strong, vicious bitch, much stronger than she looks, as has been shown in previous testimony—goes after the pimp. This pimp, kind of a little guy, looks frail, has a history of being punched out by other pimps because he's not so hot with his dukes, and if you catch him without a piece or take away his knife, a nine-year-old Puerto Rican, girl or boy, can take him.

"Okay, so she is all over him, banging him in the balls, banging his head on the sidewalk. And nobody is around to help. The whore's no fool; she split at the first blow. So what can this pimp do? He can wait until his brains have spilled into the gutter, or he can go for his knife, which he does. And mind you, he only wants to stick her enough so she'll get off him. What does he need a murder rap for? He sticks her, but she keeps on coming, she has her hands around his throat, like fucking plumber's hands, and he sticks her as hard and as far as he can. And boy, it goes in deep. Can this be anything but self-defense?"

"I didn't put it all the way in," Whipple said. "And I only cut her once."

They stared at each other.

"You think you're so smart with that hypothetical?" Whipple said dryly. "I was going to tell you anyway. I'm right up against the fucking wall, Noah. I don't give you what you want, or as much of it as there is to give, you bastards are going to let me get killed."

"If you were going to tell me anyway," Green said, "why'd you let me spin it out so long?"

"I got involved in the plot. So does the pimp get off?"

"Sure. And then the jury, joined by the judge, gives him a standing ovation. Crocker, the lieutenant has given you your rights, but I'm going to have to give them to you again. We're not funnin' anymore."

Whipple yawned as the *Miranda* warnings were tolled. "Where are you going to put me?" he asked after Green had finished.

"Don't worry. The DA does not want to lose you."

"Isolation? But how long can that be for?" Whipple took out a cigarette.

"As long as necessary. My personal, nonofficial feeling, Crocker, is you ought to get Steinberg or one of the other heavy hitters to represent you at both trials. At Barney's trial, Steinberg could make you a hero. The brave, repentant sinner. God, what balls that little man must have to go up against the Devil himself, the huge black Devil sitting right there with that earring in his ear, grinding his teeth for the day he can get at his accuser if the jury does not do its sworn duty and send the Devil away forever. Shit, they'd look at Barney and they'd look at you, and there'd be tears of civic gratitude in their eyes.

Then, at the other trial, well, you've just heard the script for that movie."

"I have to go to the john."

"You won't mind my accompanying you?" Green smiled. As he opened his office door, Green saw McKibbon, nodded and walked Whipple to the men's room. When they came back, two bottles of Dry Sack and two cups stood on the table.

"You going to break out the champagne when I sign the statement?" Whipple said.

"Anything you want, pal." Green emptied his cup in one swig and filled it again. Crocker sipped his sherry.

"Kathleen was a customer." Crocker looked at his cup. "As you know, she was—shall we say—awkward at picking up her own choices. So she'd come to me to sample my supply."

"She didn't do it at her place? Not with the professor popping in and out?"

"I have a couple of places for my clients."

"And that was you, arguing with her on the street that night?"

"Yeah."

"What was the argument about?"

"Boys. She found out, and I'd like to know from whom, that I supply boys and that, at the time, I had one living with me. She was horrified, disgusted, outraged. She said it was unnatural! Can you imagine? You have no idea what *she* did, when she could find somebody to let her do it."

"Like what?"

"You're a voyeur, Noah. In my set, she was what we call a kaka queen. You want the details?"

Green poured some more sherry. "No, thanks."

"So what *she* did was all right, but boys, that was the worst sin there was. The very worst. She said she was going to turn me in. Not to you guys, because who knew whom you took from, but to the DA. She was going to come forward even though she'd wind up on the front page of the *Post*. She could endure anything, if it meant saving those boys. I told her, when I could get a word in, that she wouldn't be saving anybody. They like it. They go after it. But she couldn't believe that."

Green filled Whipple's cup.

"Can I have some scotch after this?" Whipple asked. "Cutty Sark."

"Sure. That's the lieutenant's brand too. There's some in his office."

"Class always tells," Whipple said. "I was stewing about what Kathleen said she was going to do, and when I left her, I went to Connie's, had some drinks and kept on stewing about it. I came back."

"Weren't you afraid of waking up the professor?"

"He'd never seen me, so if he woke up and came downstairs, I had this." Whipple went into his pocket and came out with a gold badge.

"God damn!" said Green. "It looks like the real thing."

"It's a nice piece of work. It can be very useful. I'm not where I'm supposed to be and, shazam, I'm a detective."

"Where'd you get it?"

"That's not part of this deal, Noah. You're getting a lot tonight. Don't be greedy."

"Okay, but you can't keep it. It ain't legal." Green went into the desk, found some paper, wrapped the shield in several sheets, put it in an envelope and then in his pocket.

"So, she took me in the kitchen, where she was working," Whipple said. "I couldn't get anywhere with her. She was on fire. I told her I couldn't let her do it. She got nastier, and so did I. And then something really set her off."

"What?"

"I said that if she went to the DA, I'd spread the word around that the professor went for boys, the younger the better, and that's the reason she'd gone nuts on the subject. Kathleen said that would ruin her husband, that even though I had no proof—because there could be no proof—he'd be so mortified he'd have to leave the university. It's funny, I thought she didn't give a shit about him, but she did. Anyway, she went after me."

"This your scenario or mine?" Green said.

"Were you there? You want a statement, this is the statement. She could hit. Jesus. And I am not what you would call a brawler. I mean, look at me."

"I bet you could bite good," Green said amiably.

"Not if my teeth were down my throat. No, that's not my scene. Anyway, I was hurting, I really was. In the chest too. It was getting hard to breathe, and I pulled the knife. I always have it, seeing where I travel. She saw my knife and went to get one from the rack, and that's when I stuck her."

"From behind."

"Damn right. If she'd seen it coming, she could have grabbed it away. It didn't go in deep, but she passed out."

"Just like that?"

"I socked her. On the back of the head. I brought my fist down right on her. Two, three times."

"And you being so fragile, and all beat up besides?"

"Well, you know, somebody's been beating the shit out of you and you finally get a shot, you give it everything you have—you give it more than you think you have. The knife was sticking in there, and I didn't want to take it out. Messy, you know. But I wanted to make sure she wasn't going to come back at me."

"What then?"

"Well, I've never killed anybody, Noah. God knows I've wanted to, but I never could do it. But there she was, still breathing. I made sure. And I'm standing there trying to make myself finish her off. I had no choice, but I was afraid I was going to throw up all over before I killed her. Then I heard something upstairs. Jesus, he must be one of them real deep sleepers. But her falling, or something, woke him up and he called her name from upstairs. And I split."

"That's not worth Cutty Sark," Green said. "That barely gets you the house scotch."

"I'm telling you what happened. I would have killed her, but I didn't."

"Your prints?"

"I took them off the knife. Just took a second. And I didn't leave any others. I hadn't had anything to drink; I hadn't touched anything. It wasn't a social call."

"You're sure she was alive when you left?"

"That she was. That's it, Noah; it's been a long day's night."

"I'll type it up."

"Can you get me this guy Steinberg's number? I mean, after I sign. He's going to give me hell for signing anything. But I have to be safe from Barney, and this is the only way to do it. Anyway, you think I got a shot?"

"Yeah," Green said. "You got a shot. I'm not asking this because there's a connection, but are you still with us on Barney?"

Whipple nodded.

"You heard the lieutenant," Green said. "This is a very big one for us. What you do in Barney's case won't get you a recommendation from us when it comes to Kathleen."

"I figure it can't hurt. But I'd do it to Barney anyway."

"Why?"

Whipple was surprised. "What do you mean why? The motherfucker wants to kill me. Can you think of a better reason for me to ram it up his ass as far as it'll go?"

"You sound positively affectionate, Crocker."

"Say, you didn't buy what I just told you about how I left Kathleen alive, right?"

"It's not up to me. It's up to the DA."

"I want to know what *you* think. It's not like we're strangers."

Green got up, rubbed his earlobe, scratched behind the ear, sat down again and said, "Let me put it this way, whether I buy it or not, a lot of people aren't going to buy it—unless the other shoe drops."

"Well, you guys got the best clearance rate in the city, right?"

Green looked at him. "You want anything to read?"

"*Village Voice* around?"

"Oh shit, you want fiction, I'll get you some novels."

"That's crap," Lieutenant Randazzo banged his desk. "The end of it is all crap. But fuck him. Whipple put himself in the kitchen. He put the knife in his hand. That's all a jury will want to know. Still, I wish to hell you hadn't let him pull his cock out before he came."

"I believe Crocker," McKibbon said. "It's so brazen, I believe him. I'm going to see the professor bright and early."

"On what basis?" Randazzo shouted. "On what a pederast says? Yeah, go see him. But take it very easy. I want the fucking thing over with. Don't lean on him so he gets tongue-tied."

"So you *are* buying Crocker's story?" Green asked Randazzo.

"What about you?" Randazzo threw him a sour ball.

Green listened to the rain on the window for a moment. "What I think is the professor is going to be awfully relieved to see Sam."

"You know what I think?" Randazzo said. "God is punishing me because I was complaining about that hunk of meat in the river. I didn't know when I had it good. Why only two people whacking away at poor Kathleen? Maybe half the neighborhood took a whack at her. Shit. You like to clear a case nice and clean. It's not right, I should have such an awful mess."

"Death is unfair," McKibbon said.

"Very funny." Randazzo stood up. "You see, that's what happens when you have anything to do with people who fuck funny. If Kathleen had been a decent woman, she'd have been killed right."

"That's really something," Green said. "I never heard anybody get to the core of it all like that. You ought to tell that to the press when they come around."

"Are you crazy?" Randazzo snorted. "You think I want a bunch of roaring fairies dancing around my lawn?"

18 In the early evening, it was still raining, and the old man behind the bar at Rafferty's was watching the rain on the television news, along with two of his customers. The third, at the end of the bar, was crying silently.

Another old man, with long white hair, came in and nodded to the bartender. "Double gin," he said. "Water on the side."

"I know, Lieutenant." Dennis smiled as he poured.

Riordan glanced at the solitary man weeping.

"Wife," Dennis said softly. "She always said she was going to do it. She did it. No address. No nothing. Tonight, he starts off making a list of all the shows and all the movies he'd said he was going to take her to and never got around to doing. You'd be amazed how long that list was getting. He had to stop. Couldn't see anymore."

"How long's this been going on?" Riordan looked again at the weeping man.

"Lemme see—" Dennis stopped. "This is the fourth night. Hell, six months from now he'll be dreading the chance of her return."

"Maybe not." Riordan looked at the television. "He could turn into a rummy and pickle the memory of her."

"He *is* a rummy," Dennis said.

"Then he'll die alone,"—Riordan looked at the man

again—"and nobody will know he was." He smiled at the bartender. "Except you."

"Oh, they blur after a while, Lieutenant. Just like the live ones."

"You'll remember me," Riordan said.

"Oh, you're something else. You've done grand things, and you'd still be doing grand things if it wasn't for that dumb retirement rule."

"That's worth a drink." Riordan took out a five-dollar bill. "Pour yourself the good stuff."

"Thankee." Dennis took down a bottle of Johnny Walker Red and another of Tanqueray, from which he filled Riordan's glass. "The house insists."

The black anchorwoman on television announced that two murders this day—one by gun, the other by baseball bat—had broken the city's homicide record set the previous year. The shattered record had been 1,876. Now, with December not yet over, 1,878 citizens had been suddenly put to eternal rest.

"Terrible, terrible, terrible," Dennis said.

Riordan drank the double down. "What's terrible is we've gotten used to it, and we'll get used to more and more of it. You know, when I started on patrol, a murder was so horrifying a thing that everything seemed to stop when someone was killed. I mean, back then, a body lying on the sidewalk, who could look at anything else? Now, people walk right on by. Some don't even look."

"What will it all come to?" The bartender squashed his cigarette out in the ashtray.

"Fascism," Riordan said calmly. "Though it won't be called that. You can't have constitutional democracy with mad dogs, more and more of them every year, tearing at the whole fucking society. All this due process stuff—your evidence has to be gotten the right way or it gets thrown out—that's for a society of civilized people.

But if some vicious dog jumps you, you don't worry about his rights. You try to kill him before he kills you. Well, more and more, the streets are full of vicious dogs and rats and jackals. The human part of them, it doesn't function. It never did. You got nothing on you, they'll kill you. You give them what you got, they'll kill you."

"We got to bring back the chair," Dennis said.

"As a symbol of civilization, yes." Riordan took some more gin. "But the main thing," his voice became even lower than usual, "is to stop these animals from breeding. It's got to happen."

Dennis was quite interested. "How are you going to do that?"

"Oh," Riordan said, "when the decent people get enough fear inside them, they will insist that a way be found. And because it is the decent people who do the most voting, the legislatures will respond. And the courts, of course, will also follow the election returns."

"But the Church?" Dennis ignored a wave from a customer at the other end of the bar. "The Church won't stand for anything like that."

"The Church has been defeated before by the will of the people, including its own people. I tell you, Dennis, there are grand, peaceful times coming, if we live. Just like Charlie Darwin predicted."

"Who? Oh, the guy who said we come from apes."

"He said a lot more than that, Dennis." Riordan took out his wallet, extracted a slip of paper, peered at it and read: " 'Looking to the world at no very distant date, what an endless number of the lower races will have been eliminated by the higher civilized races throughout the world.' "

"You don't think it's too late, Lieutenant?" Dennis asked anxiously.

"I certainly do not." Riordan smiled at the bartender. "Who the hell do you think's got the brains, us or them?"

The crying man was singing in a low, husky voice:

If I could be with you one hour tonight,
If I could be with you, and hold you tight,
If, if, if, oh, oh Anne,
Meet me tonight in dreamland.

"Do you let him go home alone in that condition?" Riordan asked as the crying man put his head in the ashtray.

"Am I my rummy's keeper?" Dennis smiled.

Just after the next dawn, Randazzo picked up the phone and heard Green say, "Barney's given us the slip. We picked up most of the troops. Among the missing are some messengers, but we know where they're going, so we'll meet them at the other end."

"What is this slip he gave you?" Randazzo barked. "He turned himself into an Irish dwarf? Bunch of mo-rons. What'd you bring with you, a brass band?"

"He wasn't here. He wasn't at any of the places we came down on. And these cockroaches won't talk. They're more scared of him than us."

"What about the guys who were tailing him?" Randazzo said icily.

There was a pause. Then Green said, "He left them in Queens. They thought he was fast asleep."

"Jesus Christ! If I had the time, I would cry in shame. You get that Arthur?"

"Not yet."

"Not yet. Terrific. I bet you the fiddler knows where both of them are. But you still don't know where the fiddler is?"

"We're staying out until we find them all." Green raised his voice.

"Nah," Randazzo said softly. "It's gonna rain. You can't stay out there without your rubbers. Listen to me. Put Domingo on this."

"I already have."

"You're finally learning when not to listen. But watch it, Noah. Other times, you damn well better listen. I'm coming down."

That evening, Barney came out of the movie into the other darkness. Fingering the earring in his pocket, he moved in the direction of Twelfth Street, then stopped, hoping Arthur would materialize. But in the stinging cold, the streets were empty. Except for an enormous fat man in an even more enormous fur coat and a broad black felt hat. His pink face looked not so much *like* a pig's as the real thing. His eyes were nearly lost in bulges of skin, and his reddish snout was running. In a puffy, bristly hand, he held a cane pointed in front of him, occasionally poking it at the ground.

The fat man was coming directly toward Barney, who shivered and stepped into a doorway. Now, behind the fat man, a youngster in a pea jacket and earmuffs running, running so hard that, before he could stop, he ran into the fat man, knocking him to the ground.

Looking down at that face and that hand, the boy cried, "Holy shit!" and ran all the faster around the corner.

Flat on his back, the fat man, having trouble breathing, was pleading in a high, scratchy voice. "Please, I am a blind man. You can have everything I have. But please. Help me up. I am a blind man. You can have everything I have. Help me up. Please. Please."

Barney, still in the doorway, looked at him, rubbed his nose and walked away.

The fat man became silent. After a few minutes, he slowly, laboriously, raised himself, groped for the cane, found it and adjusted his coat and hat. "One was an accident," he said. "A kid. A lousy kid. What do you expect? But there was someone else. Someone breathing. Someone who said nothing and did nothing. God, create a terrible punishment for him. God, I trust you in these matters, for I know what you have done to me."

Two long blocks down Twelfth Street—in the doorway of a building across the street from a brownstone, all of whose windows were dark—Green was wishing Domingo a long, long life. In the free world.

The snitch had called the squad room four hours before, but would talk only to Green, who was not there. Domingo had, however, left a number. A pay phone. Have Green try him in half an hour, he'd said. And half an hour after that. But then the offer would expire. The number had been relayed to the command post Randazzo had set up in the back of a Chinese restaurant on Sixth Avenue. Green, under orders to phone in there regularly, picked up the message and got Domingo at the second half hour.

"Barney's got a place," Domingo had cheerily reported. "A whole fucking building. Forty-six West Twelfth. Nobody knows about it, except maybe that Arthur."

"How do *you* know about it?"

Domingo chuckled. "My people are rising in this society, Noah. They do many services, skilled services. Plumbing, carpentry, electrical work. They got fine hands. And fine eyes. They see what there is to see. Listen, you may not be in a hurry, but I am. It's getting hot down here, my friend. I think I may take a vacation. Okeydoke. Have a nice evening."

Within an hour after talking to Domingo, Green had gone through the brownstone. On the basis of the morning's busts, Randazzo had had no trouble convincing a judge that there was probable cause for a search warrant. Green found the place empty. Empty of Barney, though not of certain clothes Green recognized.

Now, across the street, Green waited, looking at the graceful front of Number 46. Two uniformed policemen were watching the back.

Finally, a tall man, without a coat or hat, walked casually past Number 46, went up to the end of the block on Fifth Avenue, disappeared and, minutes later, came up Twelfth Street once more, stopped at Number 46, walked up the stairs, took out a key, opened the door and—

"Hold it." Green, gun out, bounding across the street, noted, not for the first time, how quick he was for a man of his proportions. "Inside, Arthur," Green said, "and then stand very, very still."

"I thought you colorful gentlemen always said, 'Freeze,'" Arthur commented melodiously.

Green pushed him into the vestibule, closed the front door and said, "Okay, freeze, you scumbag." Patting Arthur down, Green extracted a Smith & Wesson .38 from a shoulder holster while silently admiring the quality of the leather.

He pushed Arthur again. "Now, inside. The bedroom at the back."

"Of course you have a warrant for this search of me?" Arthur said as they entered the room.

"A person validly arrested may be searched without a warrant," Green answered softly. "There does not need to be any indication that the person, or scumbag, arrested, possesses weapons or evidence. Although, of course, there must be probable cause for the arrest, probable cause for the search is not required. The lawful arrest, standing alone, authorizes a search. If you have pen and paper, I shall be delighted to give you the relevant citations."

"Would it be too much trouble to tell me the probable cause for my arrest?"

"Oh, there's quite a list downtown which will be revealed to you at your arraignment, sir," Green said. "As I recall, about the only complaint left out is bestiality, and that's only because the chicken wouldn't testify. Poor bird will never be the same."

Arthur moved toward a light switch.

"Oh, come on," Green said, "get your fucking hand down. Listen, Arthur, any move, any signal from here on in will be taken as an attempt to escape, and will be fatal."

"Of course," Arthur said. "That is the specialty of your profession. Killing people of color. Just for the sake of form, aren't you going to give me my rights before the execution, so that I may die with a smile on my lips?"

"Have I asked you anything yet, Miss Thing?"

"Fuck you, Jew."

"Arthur, you sit down there, I will sit down here, and we will wait for Barney. And if I hear one more word from you, I will blow your head off, starting with that ridiculous mustache."

Walking very fast, as anyone would on such a cold night, Barney, without looking to either side, went straight down Fifth Avenue without turning onto Twelfth Street.

Something funny. I got a feeling. Maybe Arthur turned. Why not? Anybody can turn. I'd give up my mama if I had to. If she was here. Anybody would give up their mama. They say they wouldn't, but they hiding from themselves. One thing I never did do. Fool myself. Shit. That damn faggot. Not enough one crazy man after my butt. Whole fucking police force is after my butt. I wasn't thinking. Should have known that Crocker could turn. Wasn't thinking because that fiddler had my whole mind. Thing is I wasn't going to kill the faggot. I thought he knew that. Just funnin' him. Why the hell did he take me seriously? Motherfucker. All rightee, got to get that fiddler off my mind so I can handle all this other shit.

Barney turned around.

That's what that feeling was. He's there. That fiddler is somewhere there. Like I figured, he followed us one day. All rightee, he's waiting to surprise me, I'm gonna surprise the life out of him. Hee, hee. And even if I don't right off, he's not going to do it wham, bam. He needs to make me crawl. Make me beg. Not wham, bam. And with just the two of us, shit, I can take him no matter what he's got on him. I can jump him. I know it. Then it's going to be wham, bam. Here I am, fiddler, come and get me.

Barney felt for the knife in his coat pocket, gripped it and turned slowly onto Twelfth Street.

No Arthur. No nobody. Then black. Black fell on him. A coat over his head. A belt or a rope or something binding his arms and pulling hard against his chest. Pulling tighter as he tried to break free. Something hard in his back.

The drawl was right behind him. "I can do it right here. You want me to do it right here? Just make any move, and I will know your wishes."

Barney stopped struggling.

"Cold must really get to you, you needing to have that coat over your head," Bama said, "but nobody going to think it strange. Not tonight. I am going to take you by the arm, and I am going to lead you where we're going, and if you change your mind and want to get it right now, you'll get it right now."

The fiddler jammed a big sweater all the way over the coat to hide the ropes. Slowly, but not gently, he guided the huge wrapped-up man back to Fifth Avenue, across it and then they turned uptown.

"My daddy knew two things real well," said the tall, lean, bearded man. "He knew every song Hank Williams ever sang, and that's a lot of songs. And he knew knots. After school, after chores were done, we'd have tying contests. Me and my brothers. On the hogs. Best practice there is, even if it's all you got. Daddy used to say you never know but one day you might have to tie some animal real good and fast. Beats clubbing them on the head. Until you're ready to. Here we are."

Parked on Thirteenth Street, near an alley at the back of the Lone Star Café, was a large, old, brown truck with no markings. The fiddler, one hand gripping the wrapped-up man, opened the front door and blew the horn twice. From the alley, Carl moved to the tailgate, let it down and the two of them pushed Barney in. The fiddler sat opposite Barney in the back as Carl started the car, and they drove off.

Had there been anyone on the street, he might have heard, from the rear of the truck, a high, sweet voice softly singing:

> *I was standing by my window*
> *On one cold and cloudy day*
> *when I saw this hearse come rollin'*
> *for to carry him away.*
>
> *Will that circle be unbroken*
> *by and by, Lord, by and by.*
> *There's a better home awaiting*
> *In the sky, Lord, in the sky.*
>
> *Undertaker, undertaker,*
> *Oh, won't you please drive slow*
> *For this body you are haulin',*
> *Lord, I hate to see him go.*

And that same passerby, had he been there, might also have heard an obligato, a deeper voice, but so muffled it was very difficult to make out the words—although, if the passerby listened hard, he might have heard this smothered antiphonal refrain:

> *Goddamn motherfucker,*
> *Goddamn motherfucker,*
> *Goddamn motherfucker.*

Randazzo was standing, looking out the window later that night, when they came in, sat down and, bracing themselves, waited.

"I used to have guys I could depend on." Randazzo had not turned around. "Not champions, but good solid guys. They had their off days, they had their good days, but they tried. Most of the time they busted their asses. They had pride. They didn't want to ever look like schmucks. So, most of the time, I didn't look like a schmuck. In fact, downtown, because our clearance rate was so high, because the morale was so high, downtown gave me a Certificate of Achievement.

"It says,"—Randazzo's back was a tower of rebuke— "I'm a 'leader in directing the efforts of detectives to achieve the optimum investigative performance, reflecting the highest ideals of professional law enforcement.' That's an absolute direct quote. And they give me a plaque to go with it."

Green and McKibbon looked at the wall opposite Randazzo's desk.

"It's not there." Randazzo was still speaking to the window. "I took it down this morning and threw it in the garbage."

The lieutenant turned around, walked slowly to his desk and sat on the edge. "Barney is gone, the fiddler is gone. The faggot is half on the pot and half off. Would one of you alleged detectives be so kind as to tell me what the fuck's going on with the professor?"

"He's been out of town," McKibbon said. "He just called me. He'll be here in half an hour. Says he has something to tell me."

"Terrific," Randazzo said. "So whatever he tells you, what have you got? The faggot put it in and maybe, just maybe, the professor stuck it in some more. So who killed her? The lawyers will take those fucking jurors and make them so *fermisht*—." He looked at the jar of sour balls with loathing. "What kind of sentence is either one going to get? What a fucking mess."

"But we got them," Green said.

"You don't listen so good," Randazzo said. "You know what? Maybe she couldn't stand being nibbled to death like that, first the faggot, then her husband, so she reached behind her and finished herself off. You ever think of that?"

The lieutenant glared at Green. "Gimme a cigar. And the other two! Place is crawling with cops. I'm down there, you're down there, and the fiddler and Barney just fly away. Way up in the sky, you can't even see them. You put a guinea in charge, and everything gets fucked up. That's what it looks like. Isn't that what it looks like? *Shut up!*"

Randazzo reached for the apothecary jar and threw it against the wall, the sour balls rolling and rolling on the floor. There was a tap on the door, a very light tap.

"Yeah?" Randazzo yelled.

Two young nuns, smiling, came in. Soundlessly, still smiling, they walked toward Randazzo's desk. He smiled too, took two dollars out of his wallet and handed the money to one of them. From a manila folder, she took out a large card and gave it to the lieutenant. There was a text, bordered with hand-colored flowers. Randazzo took the card and placed it on his desk. Still without a word, the nuns left, smiling, the lieutenant waving good-bye.

"They ought to come more often," Randazzo said. "With our luck, it couldn't hurt."

"What is it, a prayer?" Green said.

Randazzo looked at the card. "No, it's a sale on rosaries." His booming voice returned, Randazzo read, " 'He ascended to Heaven, and He will come again, this time in glory, to judge the living and the dead: each according to his merits—those who have responded to the love and piety of God going to eternal life, those who have refused them to the end going to the fire that is not extinguished.' "

"What are you looking at me for?" Green said.

" 'And His kingdom will have no end,' " Randazzo concluded.

"So Barney will get his anyway, right?" Green took out a cigar.

"That fiddler will go to the fire too," Randazzo said. "In my book, he's still the guy who took care of Tyrone. And for all we know, he's already buried Barney. Oh my God, for all we know! We don't know shit. All right, what next?"

"First we got to pray," McKibbon said.

"Fuck you!" Randazzo roared. "Fuck both of you! I liked to look at that plaque. Now, every time you see that empty space, you'll know who's responsible for it being empty."

"You really think we're lying down, Lieutenant?" Green said.

Randazzo walked back to the window. "Listen, I don't got much to enjoy these days, so let me enjoy being angry, all right?"

Twenty minutes later, McKibbon took the professor into an empty office and closed the door. Ginsburg took a chair next to the desk, and McKibbon sat in the chair behind the desk.

"As soon as I saw in the paper that this man Whipple was being charged with Kathleen's murder," Ginsburg said, "I had to come."

McKibbon nodded. "You understand, professor, that you are not in custody."

"I do. This is a voluntary confession. Would you tell me what Mr. Whipple said?"

"He used the knife only once and, he says, it did not

go in very deep. He heard some noise upstairs, so he stopped. According to him, she was still breathing."

"Yes." Ginsburg looked at the wall. "I thought she was dead. Believe me, I thought she was dead, the way she was lying there. I wanted to think she was dead, and so I told myself she was dead. She was so still. And I—I couldn't stop myself. I had this—this overwhelming need. Never in my life have I had such a need. I first took the knife out of her back and—it was all done from the back. I never saw her face. While I was doing it."

"I had a woman," McKibbon murmured, "gave me an awful hard time. I mean awful. Made me feel like a disease. I used to have fantasies about her. Fantasies about cutting her up every which way."

"I did not," Ginsburg said testily, "have such fantasies. But when I saw her lying there, I was seized by—I guess you could call it jealousy. That someone else had done this first, someone who had no *right* to. Someone she could not possibly have caused the pain, the humiliation, she had given me for so long. And I desperately wanted to be part of what had been done to her. I would not be cheated of the last satisfaction she could offer me."

"How many times?"

Ginsburg shook his head. "Many, many times."

"And then?"

"Then I wiped the handle of the knife, and I called you people."

"You figured you'd get away with it?"

"I wanted time to think. And since I am an orderly person, even under extreme stress, I remembered to wipe off the handle. That would give me time to think. I would have come to you eventually, I believe, because I cannot bear people who flinch from the consequences of their acts. But that's academic now.

"At least,"—Ginsburg was pressing the tips of his

fingers together—"she never *saw* me turn to violence; she never knew she had finally triumphed, she had finally forced me to betray my life."

"Forced you?"

"Yes. Ultimately, it was her doing. Character is fate. By what she was, she was responsible for her fate. You do understand that?"

"Up to a point, professor," McKibbon said.

"I had a terrible fear." Ginsburg was now cracking his knuckles. "I feared that, suddenly, she would turn her head, open her eyes and laugh at me. But she never moved."

"Well,"—McKibbon rose,—"we'll get this typed and then you can sign it."

"You also understand that I loved her?"

"Who would know better than you, professor?"

"I will proofread the confession before I sign it, of course."

"Of course," McKibbon said. "Oh, one thing, was she drinking coffee that night?"

"She always did," Ginsburg said. "Why?"

"There was no cup on the table."

Ginsburg nodded. "As I told you, I am very orderly; I can't stand clutter. I must have automatically put the cup in the dishwasher. But I don't understand the significance."

"There isn't any. Now. It's just something a smart old rummy I know wanted to know."

20 "How much more?" Bama called from the back of the truck.

"Ten, twelve miles," Carl said. "Some mountains, huh?"

"How the hell they ever get a road up here?"

"My people always done what had to be done. Had no choice. How's your friend?"

"Hungry," said Bama. "Ain't you, buddy?"

Barney grunted. "Got to take a shit."

"Do it in your pants." Bama looked past him.

"Hey, man, I can't walk around like that."

"You ain't walking anywhere. Up to you. Take it or hold it."

Barney sighed and looked out the back window into a jagged valley. "Where is this?"

"West Virginia." Bama lit a cigarette. "You never been here before?"

"What the fuck would I want to go to West Virginia for? *Where* in West Virginia is this?"

" 'Round Bluefield," Carl said. "Why'd you want to know? Don't mean nothing to you."

"Shit," Barney grumbled, "one thing you always got to know is where you are."

Carl laughed. "Well, where we're going's got no name."

An hour later, the truck turned off the narrow road and went up an even narrower dirt track.

"Your daddy made this?" said Bama.

"Yup. I was the one had to keep it clear though." Carl leaned forward, looking for the turning in the twilight.

The truck pulled up in front of a long wooden box with windows in it.

"Daddy," said Carl, stiffly getting out of the truck, "loved boxcars. 'Cause they traveled, you know, and he never did. Always wanted one of his own so, when he built a house, that's what he made. Can't see it in this light, but it's got the remains of a name on it. Amazing Grace Railroad. Daddy did some preaching when he was young."

Bama had the .38 out, and after Carl opened the box-car door, he pushed Barney inside. Carl put on the light, such as it was. "Damn, always meant to put in a bigger bulb." Directly before them was a large room with a sagging couch, two exceedingly well-worn armchairs, a low wooden table and a stool. To the right there appeared to be a kitchen, and to the left a series of narrow rooms that looked as if they were bedrooms for people of quite modest size.

"I'll get the stuff out of the car," Carl said, "and fix some coffee and eats."

"Not me, thanks," Bama said. "Not for him neither. We got some talking to do. After he takes his shit."

"Don't want to no more," Barney growled. "It went back in."

"It's right at home then," said Bama. "Down here." He pointed with the gun to the last of the bedrooms.

There was a faded green blanket on the bed, a chair near the window and, on the long-ago whitewashed wall, a browning newspaper photograph of a seated, straw-hatted man with a thin face, big ears, broad nose, bow tie, crisp suit and a guitar on his knee.

"Who's the silly dude?" Barney asked.

"Blues singer," said Bama.

"No way. He the wrong color."

"You never heard Jimmie Rodgers?"

"Nah."

"Ain't your fault, being culturally disadvantaged. Sit." Bama pointed to the bed.

"I ain't no dog."

"Sit. Or you're going to be a one-eared dog."

Barney sat on the edge of the bed, Bama taking the chair and moving it to the door where he stood, one foot on the chair.

"Let's start easy," the fiddler said. "Why did you kill your boy?"

Barney laughed. "Everybody know *you* took Tyrone."

"Except you and me. I'm a very good shot, sucker. I can put a lot of bullets in you and you'll still be conscious. I *know* I didn't kill Tyrone, so stop fucking around."

Barney looked at the photograph of Jimmie Rodgers.

"You had two reasons," Bama started at Barney. "One, so they'd have something on me. But the most important reason was you didn't want Tyrone saying he didn't kill Emma."

"Never was a white man who could sing the blues." Barney was still looking at the photograph. "Even if he sucked black pussy all his life."

"Emma told me. You didn't think she would. You come into the bookstore that night, the day she cut Tyrone, the day she marched into the park and got you all excited."

"We own the blues," Barney said. "We don't own much, but we own the blues."

"You told her," Bama spoke slowly, evenly, "you hadn't been with a woman for years. You didn't need a woman. A woman drains a man. Fucks him up all kinds of ways. Stays on his mind, in his mind. A woman has all kinds of power over a man, even when she's underneath him and can't move a thing. But you'd decided long ago you weren't going to let *anybody* have power over you, you weren't going to let anybody mind-fuck you when you're all alone, the way women do, the way women know so well how to do. And you'd done it, you'd really done it. Wasn't nobody could get at you all these years."

"Emma told you I said that?" Barney yawned, his fingers flexing on his knees. He looked into Bama's eyes. "Emma eat shit, Emma talk shit."

"But now," Bama stared back, "she'd fucked it up for you. She had to go and stand over you at that bench, so fine and angry, and you almost grabbed her right then."

"Too skinny. All bone. Ass like a boy."

"So you come into the bookstore that night. You come in to give her something. Something no woman had had since the time you were your own man. You could take her anytime you wanted, but you wanted her. Not just what you could grab, but *her.* And you wanted her *all* the time. And you were saying that to her, telling her how proud she should be that you had chosen her. After all those years."

Bama looked down at Barney's pants. "That's some hard-on. See, you were right all those years. They can mind-fuck you even after they're dead."

Barney lowered his arms and crossed them over his crotch.

"So you were saying all that, so excited you could hardly stand still. And what did she do? What did the chosen woman do?"

Barney took a savage nip at his thumb.

"She laughed." Bama still kept his voice even. "She stood there, fine and angry, with her boy's ass and she laughed at Barney in love. A big, loud laugh. And you moved toward her. And she said, 'You want Tyrone's knife? I'll cut your stinking balls off with it,' and she had it in her hand, and you were going to take it and grind it in her while you fucked her, but two old farts came in the door, looking for books. Books! You could have taken them too, so easy, but suddenly you remembered who you were. The big man. And it wasn't worth the odds, to blow it all there, in the open. So you skedaddled right out of there, your pecker so stiff it hurt, and behind you, she was laughing her head off."

"Emma added a whole lot, man," Barney gestured expansively. "Way women do. It was just talk, you know, jiving. Flirting, like you folks say. That's all. Wasn't no knife. Except she did show me Tyrone's in the drawer, but I didn't want it. I got much better knives than that. I get them out of the catalogues, man."

Bama was now standing. "She wasn't going to tell me because she knew I'd go cut off that ugly fat pecker. But one night, she started laughing and she couldn't stop, and I asked her what it was, and when she could talk, she made me promise on the head of the baby growing inside her that I wouldn't do anything she didn't want me to do after she told me. So she told me. And she said that was the end of it, that you would *never* come around again 'cause you could never bear to see her face again.

"And she said that I had promised, and that she didn't want me to go anywhere near you because she knew if I did, I'd kill you, and that would mean, she said, I'd never know the baby and the baby wouldn't know me, and was a piece of shit like you worth that? Well, it made sense, and anyway, we never broke promises to each other. If I'd only broken that one."

Barney, on the very edge of the bed, his body tensed, said, "She didn't tell you the whole story, sucker. I was shitting you just now. She didn't tell you I fucked her that night, after those people left. She didn't tell you I fucked her right up her boy's ass." With the last words, Barney was in the air, hurtling toward Bama, who stepped aside as Barney rammed into the wall. Coolly and carefully, the fiddler shot Barney in the kneecap.

"You all need anything?" Carl shouted from the kitchen.

"We're just fine," Bama answered, Barney on the floor howling.

"But you kept seeing her laughing." Bama was seated again, the .38 pointed at the writhing hulk. "You couldn't think of nothing else. Until you began to think that *everybody* was laughing at you, soon as you turned your back on them. So you watched, and when I left that last night, and when the house was dark, you broke in. You went right for Merle, though how you jumped him I don't know, though he is getting on. And you hid till she came in the kitchen 'cause you couldn't stand seeing her laugh at you again, and you got her in the back and you kept cutting and cutting and cutting."

"She saw me," Barney moaned. "Then she turned around to get a knife or a bottle or something, but she wasn't laughing. That bitch was not laughing."

Bama kicked him in the bloody kneecap as hard as he could. And over the screams, Bama yelled, "Nice night for a drive, Carl."

"Sure is. Be right with you. I'll bring some beer."

"Whiskey'd be better," Bama shouted back. "Oh, and bring your daddy's Bible. We'll have the whiskey after."

21 In the kitchen, where the April sun was strongest, Merle Haggard dozed. Green stepped over him to get to the table and a mug of coffee. On a plate were two bagels and a small package of Philadelphia Brand cream cheese.

"Where's the kid?" he said.

"The kid has a name. It's Joey. This is jogging day." Shannon sat down opposite him, bearing a steaming teacup.

"Does he get credit for that?"

"Sure. It's part of phys-ed. You have to pass that to graduate."

"It's a whole other world, these private schools. Christ, I didn't jog. I used to run like hell, to and from school, to avoid the daily pogrom. But it never occurred to me it ought to be part of the curriculum."

Merle Haggard slowly stretched, looking at Shannon. She rubbed the dog behind the ears, took his water dish, emptied it and filled it.

"His dish was full," Green said as he smeared cream cheese on half a bagel.

"Would *you* like to drink last night's water?"

Green looked at the dog and shook his head.

"Five months," Shannon said. "And not one lead. Just between me and you, do you think you'll ever find out what happened to Bama? And Barney?"

"I don't give up," Green said. "I've never given up on a case. You ever given up on a story?"

"Not even when it's taken away from me," Shannon smiled. "Noah, you still think somebody's going to say something somewhere, and it'll get back to you guys?"

"If it was just this city," Green said, "the odds wouldn't be all that bad. It's almost a rule. A guy who kills, he has to talk about it. To somebody he's shacking up with, or to somebody he gets good and loaded with at a bar. It may not be for years, but then, once it's out, if it's even a whisper, it may reach one of our snitches. But who the hell knows where these two went to? Or the one of them that's left. But something's got to break. I got to believe that."

"When's the professor coming up for trial?" Shannon smiled at Merle Haggard who was looking up at her.

Green sighed. "What a *tsimis.* They're still on the pre-trial motions. Ginsburg says he wants to get it over with, but his lawyer's playing games."

"Why doesn't he fire his lawyer?"

"The professor says his lawyer has every right to do what he thinks should be done, and the professor's not going to interfere with that. After all, Ginsburg did what *he* thought was right by confessing. The rest is up to the law."

"Sounds hypocritical to me." Shannon put half a slice of bagel into the toaster. "Want the other half, fatty?"

"I used to be cute."

She leaned over and roughed the detective's hair. "Cute and fat."

"The professor's not going to do any real time," Green said. "He may not do any time. The medical examiner's all *fermisht.* Crocker confesses he put it in once. Ginsburg confesses he put it in again and again and again. But how the hell can you *tell* whether the first stab did it, and all the others were free? How can you tell which *was* the first one? I wish I'd studied that stuff. I could work it out."

"But even if, somehow, you could be sure the first stab didn't kill her," Shannon said brightly, "how can you be sure Crocker was telling the truth? How do you know he didn't cut away at least as much as the professor did?"

Green stared glumly at Merle Haggard.

"So Crocker hasn't much to worry about either?" Shannon tickled Merle Haggard under the ear.

"Not in prison time. On the stuff he did with Barney, he'll probably get time served and probation. And he'll probably crawl out of this mess too."

"He's like a cockroach,"—Shannon sipped her tea— "nothing will ever kill him."

"Somebody in Barney's boys' club will. And Crocker knows that." Green thumbed his nose at Merle Haggard. "That's his sentence. That Arthur's not going away forever."

As Shannon passed his chair on the way to the sink, the detective put his hands on her hips and pulled her toward him as Merle Haggard growled softly. "How about it, smart-ass?"

Shannon looked at the kitchen clock. "You're going to be late."

Green let her go. "Damn, you're right!"

As he put on his jacket, Shannon laughed. "See! See!"

"See what?"

"The thrill is gone."

"Not in this life, kid."

"There he is," said McKibbon an hour later as they turned the corner. At one end of the park on the lower East Side was a basketball court, very much in use at the moment; next to the court, on a bare stretch of ground, lay a short, chunky man with a soft brown face. He was on his back. A kitchen knife was sticking out of his chest.

Although the players took glancing notice of Green and McKibbon, they continued the game.

"Oh Jesus," Green clenched his fist. "They got Domingo."

McKibbon shook his head and kneeled down. "He got it some time ago. Maybe last night."

Domingo looked contemplative, as contemplative as the circumstances would allow.

"It's like he expected it, like he was waiting for it," McKibbon said. "Funny. It's not his throat."

"Maybe it was too dark to be precise," Green sighed. "I'm telling you, it's like losing a relative, or worse, a friend. I really liked the little guy. Most people wouldn't know what I'm talking about, but that was a snitch with class. He took a lot of chances for us."

"And he never got busted for all those funny little pills he sold," McKibbon said.

"Yeah, well, he would have been a hell of a lot better off if he had been. Instead of being in business with us."

The detectives walked over to the basketball players, most of them Hispanic, some blacks, all in their teens or twenties.

"Hey," Green shouted, "take a break for Christ's sake!"

Only when the play in progress, culminating in a failed jump shot, was over did the players reluctantly, surlily, interrupt the game.

"Any of you guys know who this is?" Green nodded toward the corpse.

The corpse was unknown to all.

"How long's he been there?"

"Before we got here," said a tall black youngster.

"And none of you ever saw him before?" McKibbon broke in.

There was a general, indifferent shaking of heads.

"And none of us ever going to see him *again,*" one of the Puerto Rican athletes said, giggling.

"It didn't occur to any of you to report this?" Green glared at them.

The players looked as if he were speaking in some impenetrable dialect and resumed play.

"I'd like to take one of their dead mamas and put her right in the middle of that court," Green said.

"They'd just run around her." McKibbon took out his pipe. "It makes you sick."

"I'll call it in," Green said. "It's amazing somebody didn't cop his shoes."

"And the kitchen knife."

"Sam, I'm not much for the big questions, but what the hell's going to happen to this city?"

McKibbon looked at the body. "Aw, hell, Noah, what's the point of asking something like that? You just got to keep going at it each day. If you could really see ahead far enough into your *own* life, chances are you'd slit your throat. And you want to know what's going to happen to this whole fucking city?"

"What I mean is, I'd like to have a kid, you know, and I ain't got that much time. But to bring a kid into this?" Green looked at the corpse and then at the players.

McKibbon laughed. "Shit. Suppose your great-grand-father, back in the old country, looked around and saw all the Jew-haters breeding more Jew-haters, and suppose he said, 'Fuck it, you've had enough victims.' You wouldn't be here."

"And if they'd all said that, there wouldn't have been a Holocaust." Green took out a cigar.

"Been a lot of Jews alive since then," McKibbon said,

"and even digging it. You even got your own country since then."

A thin black girl, about fourteen, walked past and stopped, her eyes on the players who were totally involved in their own action. "There were three of them," she whispered quickly. "That's all I could see. It was late. Around one o'clock or so."

"You wouldn't know their faces?" Green talked to the girl as McKibbon stood in front of them, blocking them from the players' view.

"No," the girl said.

"Were they big? Some tall, some short?"

"It was dark. I'm not sure. They were all men."

"You didn't hear anything?"

"No. I saw him fall, and they ran away."

"Was anybody else around?"

"No, I don't think so."

"Where can we find you?" McKibbon asked gently.

"I told you everything. Good-bye." And she ran away.

McKibbon and Green looked at each other. "Nothing to it," McKibbon said. "We know they're male. The rest is just a process of elimination."

"Damn!" Green sat down on a bench and reached for a cigar. "There's got to be a connection between those three guys the girl saw and Stubblefield—and those *bodega* killings."

"How the hell do we know? We never moved an inch on those two cases," McKibbon said. "You know that's the way it comes down sometimes. Quiet as it's kept, you can get away with murder. Sometimes."

"It was us. We couldn't get the beginning of a handle on either one of them." Green was staring in front of him. "I kept hoping Domingo would finally say something. I guess I wasn't the only one with that expectation."

Green stood up. "I want this one, Sam."

McKibbon nodded.

"As long as it takes," Green said, "it's mine. Official or not."

They walked in silence for a couple of minutes. "Say," McKibbon said, "I just remembered. You *got* to have a kid. Who's going to say *Kaddish* for you?"

Green stopped, frowned and said, "That makes no sense. I never understood it. You're dead, you're dead. What the hell good is somebody saying prayers for you then?" He looked at McKibbon and grinned. "But you know, I guess I would like that."

"See," McKibbon poked him in the shoulder, "there's always something to look forward to."